Race A...

In another moment we were beyond the rim of light and into night. Rowena, who knew the route, took the lead. Fortunately, the moon was out. It silvered the white Haseley Hall fences and the dark ones of Unicorn Farm. Beauvais galloped surely, and it came to me that he, too, knew this route very well, that Rowena must have been riding him between the two farms for some time.

It came to me, too, that Rowena was very much afraid—not of this ride, but of what she would find at its end....

Bantam Starfire Books by Norma Johnston
Ask your bookseller for the books you have missed

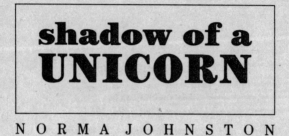

shadow of a UNICORN

NORMA JOHNSTON

BANTAM BOOKS

TORONTO • NEW YORK • LONDON • SYDNEY • AUCKLAND

RL 6, age 12 and up

SHADOW OF A UNICORN
A Bantam Book / May 1987

*Starfire and accompanying logo of a stylized star are
registered trademarks of Bantam Books, Inc. Registered
in U.S. Patent and Trademark Office and elsewhere.*

ISBN 0-553-26475-3

Published simultaneously in the United States and Canada

---

*Bantam Books are published by Bantam Books, Inc. Its
trademark, consisting of the words "Bantam Books" and
the portrayal of a rooster, is Registered in U.S. Patent
and Trademark Office and in other countries. Marca
Registrada. Bantam Books, Inc., 666 Fifth Avenue, New
York, New York 10103.*

PRINTED IN THE UNITED STATES OF AMERICA

O   0 9 8 7 6 5 4 3 2 1

For Kimberley,
who will one day
own a unicorn farm.

Whenever I remembered Unicorn Farm, I remembered sunlight. I could close my burning eyes and see it all again . . . the six-year-old that I'd been then, skipping along between my father and our cousin Rowena Drake to the paddock where Beauvais was grazing. Beauvais, Rowena's pride and joy, who two months before had almost won the Kentucky Derby. The white star on his forehead had blazed in the sunlight, and his bay coat had gleamed. The white paint of Kentucky's traditional white fences had shimmered. The very air had shimmered in the bright July afternoon, from off in the apple orchard came the drowsy hum of bees, and suddenly, with an almost unbearable sharpness, I had been overcome with a sense of happiness and peace.

Now it was August, ten years later. The air in our Connecticut apartment—*my* apartment now, my mind corrected dully—was just as hot and still but far more suffocating. The buzz that came distantly was not the hum of bees but the voices of my relatives deciding my future without consulting me. I was lying on my back in my small, familiar bedroom, staring out the window at the blank-faced apartments opposite, and all at once, so clearly that I could have reached out and touched it, I saw a vision of blue sky and sunlight. A gracious red-roofed house with tall white pillars. I could almost hear Beauvais whinny, and smell the flowers along the graveled paths, and feel the peace. I saw Dad lifting me onto Beauvais's back while Mother and Uncle Gil snapped pictures, and Dad held me steady, and Rowena and Aunt Roberta looked on, laughing.

It was so real, and so unattainable, that it broke my heart. Because Dad had been dead, from a car crash, for six years. Uncle Gil and Aunt Roberta had been dead for two, of an even more shocking accident—a fire that had swept through Unicorn Farm's stables, destroying half their stock. Mother had been dead four days.

Four days—was that all it was? In a way, it seemed forever. That was probably because I'd been anticipating losing her throughout the six months since the doctors had said further chemotherapy would do no good. I hadn't cried, not once.

On the other side of the thin wall that separated the bedrooms from the living room, the voices of my relatives went on, trying to solve the problem of "what's to become of Sarah." Mother hadn't told her brother Hugh about her cancer, and her death had been a shock. He and his second wife were worrywarts, health nuts, and hypochondriacs. They were probably never going to forgive me for not telling them, despite Mother's wishes. I hadn't told my grandfather Burton, either, but *he* hadn't scolded me; he'd just hopped on a plane and flown up from

New Mexico as soon as I'd phoned him that Mother had died.

I wished I could go back to New Mexico with him, but I knew I couldn't. He was in his eighties, and he didn't have room or need the additional responsibility. That left, as I was all too unpleasantly aware, Uncle Hugh and Aunt Alicia. As soon as we'd returned to the apartment from the cemetery, they'd begun discussing me in my presence, as if I were a piece of family furniture that needed to be stored someplace, no one knew where.

I'd fled to my bedroom before I could say something I'd regret, but the family conference had continued. How Mother would have hated it! No, her eyes would have twinkled, and she'd have launched into a devastatingly funny mockery of Uncle Hugh's pompous style. How we'd have laughed!

I ached to hear that laughter. What I heard instead was Uncle Hugh lecturing about "an excellent boarding school," and a wave of nausea engulfed me.

Somehow, Mother and I had never discussed what would become of me "after." We hadn't talked about the cancer, either. There had been too much else we'd rushed to share while we had the chance. Since Dad's accident, Mother and I had been a self-sufficient family unit, and quite happy, really. We'd had to sell the house (which I hadn't minded much), sell my pony (which had broken my heart), and move from almost-country to small city. Mother had gone to work (and done well) and I to a new school (where I'd done pretty well too). When I was younger, I'd gone to camp (one with horses); since I'd been in high school, I'd had summer jobs (not with horses, to my regret). There had been vacations, even a trip to Europe. Basically, life had been fun up until Mother's illness had struck. Even then, she'd gone down fighting.

Now *I* had to fight if I wanted to escape Uncle Hugh's plans. But not right now. I didn't want to fight yet. I wanted peace and quiet. I wanted Rowena, but she wasn't there. I hadn't seen Rowena for three years, but I still clung to the memory of how I had adored her. I needed her now, desperately, but she hadn't called, though I'd telegraphed and left messages twice on her answering machine. She hadn't shown up at the funeral this morning, or at the cemetery afterward, as I'd unconsciously expected.

I rolled over, staring out the window at the muggy sky, and wished that I could cry.

And then the telephone rang.

"Sarah? Oh, darling, I'm so sorry but I only just got your messages. I'm up at Saratoga; I've had one of Beauvais's grandsons entered in the races, and I have a two-year-old up for sale—"

It was Rowena. At the sound of that unmistakable voice, like organ chords, a picture of her rose vividly . . . hair the color of dark honey and dark eyes like mine; an athlete's grace, because for a few years she'd been a jockey. Rowena said warmly, "Sarah, I'm so sorry. I wish I'd known. Love, I wish I could jump on a plane right now and come to you, but I just can't. Is it very grim? Can you hold up all right for a few days till I can get there?"

I drew a shaky breath. "It's awful. And I may not *be* here in a few days. Uncle Hugh's busy making plans to close up the apartment and ship me off to boarding school. I don't know where he expects to park me till school starts, except it's probably not with him. Which is just as well. I might commit double murder!"

Incredibly, like a welcome breath of air, I heard Rowena laugh. "You march in there and tell that old iceberg what he can do with his boarding school! You're coming to Unicorn Farm. Your mother and I worked it all out by telephone six months ago. Yes, she told me about the cancer," she went on as I caught my breath. "I just didn't know the end was so close or I'd have told you where to reach me."

Her bluntness cut through my fog of grief like a surgeon's knife, and I blessed her for it. "Your mother appointed me your legal guardian," Rowena went on more gently. "She sent me notarized papers, and it's in her will. Her lawyer will probably be telling you all about it in a day or so, but you might as well have the pleasure of letting Hugh know right now. Sarah, I can't leave Saratoga for two more days, and it really would be best for me to go straight to Kentucky. Can you stick it out till Friday? And do you think you can manage to get down to Lexington on your own?"

"I'd manage if I had to walk every step," I said fervently. "Oh, Rowena, you don't—" I stopped and swallowed. "I can't—imagine anywhere I'd rather be right now than Unicorn Farm."

"It may not be quite the safe haven you remember." There was a note in Rowena's voice I could not identify, but I didn't think about it then. I said good-bye and went, with bitter satisfaction, to inform my uncle that his orphan niece was off his hands.

It wasn't till I was on the plane to Lexington three days later, on the Friday Rowena had suggested, that it dawned on me. For all the warmth there had been in Rowena's voice, for all the love and tenderness that it contained, the one thing that had not been there was a sense of peace.

I flew on Friday afternoon into a Lexington boxed in by lowering clouds. It was so strange. The flight south was through a sky of brilliant blue, alive with sunshine, with a carpet of white clouds below. It had continued to be muggy in Connecticut, with storms threatening, and not just in the weather. My uncle and aunt, though relieved to have me off their hands, had also had ten fits over not having been consulted.

Grandfather Burton left on Thursday after telling me: "You need me for anything, you get on the phone, you hear?" I nodded and kissed him goodbye gratefully. I would have kissed my aunt and uncle off with enormous gratitude if they'd only gotten into their rented car and left me to spend my last night in the Connecticut apartment alone with memories. No such luck—they knew their duty, and they did it, right down to hiring a van to pick the furniture up for storage, and arranging for the apartment to be sublet. I spent the last night packing my clothes in suitcases, and putting other personal belongings into cartons for shipping south. At least I was too busy cursing my aunt and uncle to miss my mother.

It wasn't till I was in the Piedmont Airlines plane above the clouds that the sun's rays, bouncing off the wing, played tricks upon my mind and I started seeing, not the present, but the future and the past. And it was weird. I conjured up the picture of Unicorn Farm and saw it again as I remembered it—the sunlight, and the peace, and the red-roofed Greek Revival mansion. And the great bay stallion in the far pasture, and the figures walking toward him. I could see a ray of sun dancing off Beauvais's white blaze, up and out, almost like a unicorn's horn.

Years ago, maybe it was on that first visit, I asked my mother, "What's a unicorn farm?" And Mother had explained that the farm was named for a mythical beast, a horse with a single, twisted horn.

That was the year Beauvais almost won the Derby—he'd taken a fall, injuring his leg, while coming down the home stretch—and people were talking about him as a wonder horse who'd been mysteriously struck down. Somehow or other I'd gotten it into my six-year-old head that Beauvais was, or had been, a unicorn. Rowena had laughed and said that Beauvais, like a unicorn, had brought the farm good luck. Because miraculously, Beauvais hadn't had to be destroyed. His leg had healed, and even though he could no longer race, he was "at stud," busily and happily siring other racehorses as fast as he could.

I could picture Beauvais when I pictured Unicorn Farm, but I could not yet see myself there. I had another year of high school to finish, but I flinched from the prospect of entering a new school as a senior. Should I get a job? I wondered. As what?

Face it, I told myself bluntly. I didn't know *what* I wanted, other than to lose myself in Unicorn Farm.

At that moment, the plane started jouncing down, jolting my stomach as it broke through the clouds. The Kentucky landscape spread below me, oddly grayed . . . no rain, but a gloomy stillness, unusual in midafternoon. I saw the miles of fences with their traditional four rails, the stallion paddocks next to one another but not touching, so that each stallion was separated by twenty feet of grass from his neighbor rival. I saw the toy village, white and red, that was the famed Calumet Farm, right by the airport.

Then the plane touched down, and people started pushing into the aisles, and I was swept into the bustle of landing and claiming luggage. It was the first time I'd flown alone, but I scarcely had time to be aware of that.

I retrieved the last of my suitcases and looked around for Rowena, but she wasn't there. Instead, as the crowd thinned, there was a large elderly man bearing down on me.

"You must be Sarah. You look like a Burton. Spitting image of your great-aunt Roberta. I'm your great-uncle Gil's brother Ned. Dr. Edward Drake, if you insist on being formal. Come along, young lady. I'm parked in a loading zone, and it would be just like one of those young whippersnappers to ticket me."

He took the luggage cart from me and started

off, leaving me to hurry after him across the lobby. "Where's Rowena?" I called breathlessly.

"Not back from Saratoga yet. Getting in sometime later this afternoon. Good thing I saw your flight information on her calendar, or you'd have been left here stranded," he trumpeted back, barreling toward the swinging door. I marveled that he moved so quickly. It wasn't just his age and girth, it was his—disorganization, that was it. He looked like one of those monumental old ruins in a TV western.

We reached the loading zone just as a uniformed motorcycle officer was about to write a ticket. Dr. Drake promptly sounded off at him. The officer gave a rueful sigh. "Suppose you'd just file it with the rest of them," he said, tearing the ticket up. He grinned at me and puttered off. Dr. Drake began slinging my suitcases haphazardly into the trunk of the battered Chevy.

At that moment, making me think again irresistibly of a TV show, a van raced between the sawhorses blockading what was once a parking lot and was now a construction site. A tanned young man with a thatch of brown hair leaned out the window, gesturing to me wildly.

I blinked as he braked with a screech and jumped out. "No, you don't!"

It wasn't me he was addressing, it was the doctor. He was removing my suitcases firmly as the older man sputtered and protested. "I'm supposed to collect Sarah. Miss D phoned and told me to. And the vet's going to be here to meet the boss's flight, so you don't have to hang around for it. She'd better hear about Dancer from him first, got it?"

I didn't know what he meant. I did know a duel

of wills was going on, between the doctor's eyes and the young man's, and it was the young man who won. The doctor's shoulders sagged slightly inside the rumpled suit, and the young man turned to me curtly.

"You ready to go? Come on."

He wasn't being rude, he simply wanted to get out of there. And suddenly I did too.

I climbed into the front seat of the van and we pulled off, spraying gravel, almost before my door was closed. When we were out of the airport, on the main road, he slowed and gave me a crooked, attractive smile. "I'm Tim Payne. I'm a stallion groom, and right now I'm your cousin's errand boy. Sorry about that, but it was exactly the situation she wanted you to avoid."

"Was he drunk?" I asked baldly.

Tim looked at me with respect. "You don't beat around the bush, do you? Officially Doc's been on the wagon for years, but who knows? You'd have been safe enough with him behind the wheel, but Rowena didn't think you needed an overdose of moonshine and magnolias right off the bat."

So my cousin was Miss D to Tim in the doctor's presence, but Rowena in private. "You sound as if you know Unicorn Farm pretty well," I murmured.

"No. I'm from Upstate New York. Just working at Unicorn while I go to the university here." Abruptly, and for no reason I could fathom, he turned cold. That was the last thing Tim Payne said until we were on Ironbridge Pike and swinging through the high wrought-iron gates of Unicorn Farm. At that moment, a ray of sun broke through the clouds, gilding the fanciful figure atop the arch. A horse, prancing, with a single horn . . . my eyes, though dry, stung suddenly.

When I opened them, Tim was saying in quite an altered tone, "Welcome to Unicorn Farm, Sarah Burton. I know that's what Rowena would say if she were here."

And then we were sweeping up the graveled drive, and the manor house loomed before us on its slight rise. White-pillared, gracious, with its spreading porches, three stories of tall windows, and a red mansard roof. There were baskets of fuchsias, and of white geraniums and raspberry-colored petunias hanging from the porch eaves. And white wicker furniture with raspberry cushions—Unicorn Farm's racing colors—just as I remembered.

Only the ray of sun had vanished. It was odd, I couldn't remember ever having seen Unicorn Farm in shadow.

Tim jumped from the driver's seat and came around to open my door. I stepped down slowly.

As I did so, a tall, pear-shaped figure came shambling along the gravel path from the stables. *Cyrus*—I had forgotten all about him, yet now the memory came back sharply, even though I couldn't recall his last name. Cyrus, Beauvais's groom, who'd come to Unicorn Farm as a stable boy in Rowena's grandfather's time. He must be nearly eighty now, I calculated quickly. My mind's eye remembered the papery pink-and-white old face, the piercing eyes of faded blue, even before he was close enough for me to see them. Whether he remembered me, I couldn't tell. My greeting died on my lips as he spoke to Tim succinctly.

"It don't look good. You better come."

Tim stiffened. Then he was off down the gravel path. I pelted after him and caught at his arm.

"What is it? Not Beauvais—"

He jerked around as though he'd forgotten my existence. Then his eyes focused. "Not this time. It's Bright Dancer, Rowena's steeplechaser. She's come down with some kind of virus or bacteria. Look, go through Rowena's phone book and call the vet for us, will you? His name's Voelkner. Tell him to get out here fast, that I'll meet Rowena's plane for him. Sorry about your luggage. It'll have to wait."

He took off at a gallop as I slowed, staring after him. Then I turned and started back toward the manor house, thinking hard. The gray afternoon was fading into unnaturally early twilight, and Cyrus was no longer in sight. I pulled the nearest suitcase out of the van and took it with me up the broad steps. The carved front door, with its leaded glass fanlights and sidelights, was not ajar in the old hospitable pattern. It was locked, probably because Rowena'd been away. I left my suitcase on the porch and tried two other doors before finding the slanting trapdoor to the cellar unlocked. That was how I got in.

The house lay in shadow. I was vaguely conscious of the carved white paneling and old Oriental rugs, the double parlors, with their Victorian mahogany and raspberry-colored silks, just as before. I headed for the library that had been my uncle's study, all white and gold, and my heart was hammering. It was Rowena's office now. Ledgers were piled on the big double desk before the fireplace, with notes in her handwriting inserted in them.

I switched on the desk lamp, and a shadow

leaped onto the far wall, looming over me. The shadow of a unicorn—I almost shrieked until, almost at once, I realized it was cast by a small brass statuette on the desk. Feeling silly, I looked for the phone book, found Dr. Voelkner's number, and punched it quickly. He asked questions that I couldn't answer, then curtly told me which buttons to push to transfer the call out to the stable.

I obeyed. Then I went through the downstairs rooms, lighting lamps, so Rowena would not return to a forsaken house as well as a sick horse. I retrieved my suitcases and lugged them up the mahogany staircase one by one. I took for granted Rowena would put me in the room I'd always had here, the rose-spangled Victorian one behind her own. Sure enough, a welcoming bouquet of real roses stood in a crystal vase on the dressing table. Who had picked them in Rowena's place—Tim? I had no idea what the help situation was at Unicorn Farm, but obviously there was no live-in housekeeper, as in the old days.

I wanted to go out to the stables, but something held me back. Something was going on there that I wasn't part of; I was still an outsider here. So I unpacked, putting my clothes carefully into the closet and the Chippendale highboy. In the lower hall the grandfather's clock ticked loudly . . . five o'clock; five-thirty. Some time ago a car, probably the vet's, had streaked into the drive and around back to the stables. Now the Unicorn Farm van, with Tim presumably at the wheel, tore out. There was no sign of Dr. Drake.

The van returned and went straight past the house. I looked out the back windows of my room and could see, far out past the orchard, the rambling bulks of the stallion and broodmare barns. Ordinarily, at this time of year, the horses spent the night in their pastures, being brought in only during the day's worst heat.... Tonight, lights glowed from windows in the second barn. More light poured from the open door. A slim figure I took to be Rowena's catapulted from the van and ran inside.

One of Unicorn Farm's valuable horses was gravely ill, though not Beauvais. *Not this time.* That was what Tim had said. It made no sense, but it made a chill run through me.

I sat down in the rocker by the bedroom fireplace and locked my hands around my knees. In a kind of flashback, I was sitting again in the waiting room of the Hartford hospital, hearing Mother's doctor tell me with brutal kindness that there was no use waiting, there was no use hoping.

Again, I could not cry, but my eyes burned and my throat was very tight. All the bones in my body ached. I had run to Unicorn Farm as a port in a storm, but it was, as Rowena had warned me, no safe haven. Over the remembered peace a shadow fell, like the shadow of the unicorn cast on the study wall. And it touched me. It was not something I had brought with me in my grief; it had bred and grown here; it had touched me and would touch me more because I was now a part of Unicorn Farm.

I was so sure of those things that when much later the front door opened and I walked out and down the stairs to face Rowena, I knew before she spoke what she would say.

She stood there in the pool of light from the crystal chandelier, still in her pale linen suit, wrinkled now and flecked with straw. Her tawny hair was skewered up every which way, and her dark eyes were filled with pain and with compassion.

"Sarah, love . . . I'm sorry that I wasn't around for you, that you had to arrive to *this*." She made an inconclusive gesture. "Bright Dancer died. But oh, my love, I *am* so glad *you're* here."

She held out her arms to me, and I went to them. She was my guardian, but I had the oddest feeling, as we hugged, that it was I who was needed to take care of her.

CHAPTER

3

"I was planning to take you out to dinner, somewhere cool and restful. But it's gotten so late . . . on a Friday night everyplace will be crowded." Rowena smiled at me wearily. "To be honest, I don't feel like making the effort. Do you mind?"

"Of course not," I said resolutely. "*I'll* cook something."

"No, you will not. You've had enough house-keeping, and everything else, lately. We'll phone for pizza or something after I've showered and changed. No, I'd better check my messages before anything." Rowena moved into the library, and I followed. The answering machine tape was full and I listened to it silently as Rowena, too restless to sit down, paced back and forth making notes on a small pad. There were the messages I'd left, my voice growing increasingly strident. After the third one, Rowena looked across at me sadly.

"Sarah, I'm *so* sorry."

"Don't be silly! There was nothing you could

have done. And you did find out right when it really
mattered."

"Oh, yes. Uncle Hugh." Rowena's lips twitched.
"You'll have to fill me in on him while we eat."

"*You'll* have to fill *me* in on *that,*" I said point-
edly a short time later. The tape had reached today's installment of messages and for the fourth
time a male voice, somewhat accented, somewhat
imperious, demanded, "Rowena, what is going on?
Am I taking you and your ward to dinner this evening, or am I not? I am becoming impatient. Also
hungry."

"That's Greg. I'd better phone him," Rowena
said briefly. But a faint color rose in her face and
her lips curved slightly. She snapped off the answering machine and punched a number. "Mr. Stahl,
please. It's Miss Drake . . . Greg, I'm sorry, we'll
have to take a rain check. I've been out in the barn
ever since I got back." Her voice wavered, then
firmed. "Greg, I've lost Dancer . . . we don't know
yet, but it looks like that same bacteria. Just *snap!*
like that. The fever only started last night."

I looked at the shadow of the unicorn statuette
against the wall. It loomed there, oddly ominous.
Rowena murmured a few more inaudible sentences
and put down the phone.

"That's that. The rest of the messages can wait
till morning. Are you settled in your room all right?
Come up with me while I change."

We went up the broad staircase together arm in
arm. Rowena's room was in the front, to the left as
you faced the manor house from outdoors. Between
it and the other front bedroom was a small sitting
area, set apart from the rest of the hall by pillars,
that the family called the "foyer." Light spilling from

the hall lantern vaguely showed the shabby blue velvet couch and easy chairs that I remembered. Rowena glanced toward the closed door of the other front bedroom. "No light on. Uncle Ned's not home."

"He met me at the airport." I felt embarrassed. "He sort of—took off after Tim Payne told him he wasn't wanted. He hasn't come in; I'd have heard."

"Rude but accurate," Rowena said, referring to Tim's message. She went into her own bedroom, gesturing for me to follow. I sat down on a chair covered in the same brown and coral chintz that rambled over walls, windows, and the four-poster. "I'd meant to break Uncle Ned to you gently. You must have heard of him, but all the same, he can be rather disconcerting in the flesh."

"Does he live here?"

"He still keeps an apartment up by Aqueduct Race Track in New York, but judging from appearances, he's making this his permanent home. He came on a visit, to help me, after the fire, and he just stayed."

"And he's a doctor?" It didn't fit well with what I'd seen and heard this afternoon.

"Let's save that for later. I'm not up to explaining Uncle Ned on an empty stomach." Rowena pulled off her suit and blouse and opened a door in the wall beside the fireplace. "There's a new bathroom that we'll share, where the old closets used to be, did you notice? I stole space from the hall linen closet for our new closets. With a door in their connecting walls, just like the old ones had. So you see, I was expecting you to come back to visit!"

Except that this was not just a visit.... I leaned back in the chair and put my feet up on the hassock, and the weariness of the whole past week engulfed me. Faintly, I could hear the sound of the shower, then that, too, faded. The next thing I knew, Rowena was bending over me in compassionate amusement.

"Which would you really rather do, eat or sleep?"

"Eat," I said firmly. "And hear about"—was I imagining things, or did Rowena involuntarily brace herself as though a cold current had come into the room?—"about Greg Stahl," I substituted for the other, more serious things I had been about to say.

Rowena's eyes danced. "Gregory Stahl is half-English, half-Swiss, and all gorgeous. He had a Kentucky grandmother, I believe. He's also rich! He bought Haseley Hall from the Lattimers when old Mr. Lattimer couldn't afford to keep it up anymore." A shadow flitted across her face. "Anyway," she went on briskly, tightening the sash of her terry-cloth robe, "Greg's done wonders with the place. Computerization, scientific breeding methods, and all that. He's poured a fortune into it, and now the business is geared up for expansion."

"So he's all ready to take over Unicorn Farm, Beauvais, and Rowena Drake, not necessarily in that order?" I inquired dryly.

Rowena blushed. "Sarah Burton, you always have been too perceptive!"

"Is that why you let me come here?"

I meant that jokingly, but the words hung in the air, taking on added meaning. Then Rowena pulled me to my feet. "Come on! Have you forgotten that we're both famished?"

We ran downstairs and out back to the kitchen. *That* was a surprise. The old-fashioned room that I remembered had been replaced by a much larger one that was old-fashioned in decoration only. The

vinyl floor looked like old brick; real brick formed
most of the walls. The numerous cupboards looked
Colonial, and the long trestle table and Windsor
chairs really were. But there were stainless steel
double sinks, and built-in ovens, and a big refrigerator-
freezer. And a microwave above the built-in stove.
And a fireplace, with a couch and rocker. And in
the microwave a casserole giving forth a savory
aroma.

A note stuck to the ventilator hood said: *This
was one of my better efforts. Wasn't it lucky I had
some left over in my freezer? See you guys tomorrow. T.P.*

Rowena shook her head. "That Tim! It wasn't
luck, it was inevitable that he'd have leftovers. He
always cooks too much. Some great, some awful."
She took the casserole out and sniffed critically.
"He's right, this is one of the better ones. It *was*
nice of him, and even nicer that he didn't stick
around."

"Rowena, who *is* he?"

"Tim? He's a student in the university's equine
management program. I chose him out of a group of
applicants for the groom position, and he's been
great. Like last night, when he discovered something was seriously wrong with Dancer.... He grew
up in New York State somewhere, and obviously
loves horses. Other than that, I don't know." Rowena's eyes narrowed. "Why do you ask?"

"I don't know." I did know, though: Something
had seemed strange. The way he'd gotten rid of Dr.
Drake; the way his walls had gone up when I asked
about him and Unicorn Farm. And the look of alarm
that had been in his face when he'd seen Cyrus
coming. It wasn't just because of Dancer's illness.

Something told me it was more . . . just as something held me back from saying that to Rowena.

I'd never felt scared at Unicorn Farm before, and it jolted me. I'd never felt hesitant of saying things to Rowena before, that was another jolt. I sat there in the expensive kitchen, watching Rowena move quietly around, taking out plates and silver.

Then Rowena turned and smiled at me. "Did you have anything halfway decent for lunch on the plane?" she asked. "I'm sorry I didn't give you a proper dinner at the proper hour."

"It doesn't matter."

"But it does. I wanted to make Unicorn Farm be everything you remembered."

"It couldn't be that anyway," I said quietly.

For a moment an image of the past, with both our sets of parents present, shimmered in the lamplight. Rowena looked away. I swallowed hard.

"I'm sorry about Dancer," I said thickly.

Rowena turned back and, deliberately, smacked her hand against the table. "Let's make a pact. No more apologies, and no more condolences. And no more walking on eggs. Okay?"

"Okay." I took a deep breath. "How come there's no housekeeper here anymore? You don't have enough to do running the stables, or you've suddenly turned domestic? Or is something weird happening on the farm that you haven't told me?"

Rowena looked at me sharply. "What prompted that?"

"No housekeeper. The farm's white fences have turned black with creosote. I remember Uncle Gil telling me that would save money, but he'd never do it. But you have. And the flower gardens along the driveway needed weeding." I shrugged uneasily.

"Things just feel—queer. And what you said on the phone—about Unicorn Farm not being a safe haven. What's happened, Rowena? Has the bottom dropped out of the thoroughbred market? Or have all your stallions suddenly gone sterile?"

I was speaking faster, and a lot more bluntly, than I'd ever talked to Rowena before. Because I was older now; because the tragedies we'd each gone through had aged us both and also brought us closer. Because of what suddenly, sharply, had become clear to me: Unicorn Farm's income depended on its success as a stud and breeding business, and Unicorn Farm was going through a money shortage. That was obvious, now that I thought about it, in the subtle shabbiness that had stolen in everywhere.

"Where did you get that about the stallions?" Rowena demanded.

I did a double-take. "Nowhere. It just occurred to me. Rowena!" In my embarrassment I attempted a not-so-funny joke. "You don't mean Beauvais and his pals have suddenly lost interest in the birds and the bees?"

"Interest has nothing to do with ability in the horse business," Rowena said with equal frankness. "If you ask Doc Voelkner, he'll mumble about bacteria or viruses. If you ask old Cy, he'll tell you Unicorn Farm has a curse on it."

4

"That's crazy!" I blurted out after a stupefied silence.

"Of course it is, but who says something must be rational to be believed?" Rowena went to the microwave and took out Tim's casserole. "Here. Eat. If you wait till I've told the whole story, you may lose your appetite."

"That's what you think," I muttered, digging in. I served her, then myself; speared a forkful of something resembling moussaka, and looked her in the eye. "All right. Tell."

Rowena tasted and raised a respectful eyebrow. "Definitely one of Tim's better efforts. You're right, Sarah, and I might have known you'd spot it right off the bat. Unicorn Farm *is* in trouble. I probably should have warned you before I let you come."

"Financial trouble?" I asked.

"That, of course. But not just that." Rowena ran her fingers through her hair. "You'd better let me tell this in chronological order, or it won't make sense." She ate rapidly for a few minutes, then continued. "It started with the fire . . . when I took over ownership under Dad's will. A lot of people thought I wouldn't be able to run the business on my own. Particularly after the fire losses. Some of our best breed stock, and three stallions that were being boarded here, were killed. None of our own stallions, thank the Lord. But three yearlings that we were going to put up at the Fasig-Tipton Winter Sale died from smoke inhalation; and two more were burned and had to be put down." She broke off for a moment. "If the fire had only been in summer! In summer the horses stay out all night; they're only brought in during the day's worst heat. . . . But of course, in the summer the fire wouldn't have broken out."

"I never have understood just what happened."

Rowena shrugged. "The police still aren't completely sure. One of the space heaters seemed to have been defective. Or the cat knocked over one of the kerosene lanterns. You remember old Mittens. She was one of the fire casualties too."

"But it *was* an accident?"

"Oh, yes," Rowena said quickly. *Too* quickly? I must have frowned, for Rowena added, "Sarah, don't go imagining anything! Even the insurance firms decided it was an accident. They paid off the owners of the dead stallions, and they paid full coverage on what we'd lost. Of course, that didn't come close to covering replacement costs. Starting up again, without Dad at the helm . . . a lot of people just assumed I'd have to put Unicorn Farm on the market."

"Including Gregory Stahl?" I asked casually.

"Oh, Greg had been after Dad to sell to him for over a year. He needs more land, and he'd like to own at least a share of Beauvais. But Dad was determined not to syndicate our stallions, or to sell off any acreage. He said, 'Drakes have owned this land and the horses on it for over a hundred and fifty years, and nobody but Drakes will ever own even a share of it.' I think Greg understands that better than he'll admit," Rowena finished wryly. "He wheels and deals like mad, but you should see the expression on his face if anyone asks why he hasn't sold the dilapidated English cottage that's been in his family for generations!"

"It started with the fire, you said. What started?"

"Accidents," Rowena said simply. "Maybe I should say catastrophes."

She bit her lip. Rowena had dimmed the kitchen work lights when we began to eat, and the room was half in shadow. The green-shaded kerosene-type lamp above the table made her face look strained and older. There were faint lines and hollows underneath her eyes.

I took a swallow of water, and my voice came out flat and matter-of-fact.

"Maybe you should say they weren't all accidents."

There, it was out . . . the thing I'd been thinking ever since I'd arrived.

A look of relief flitted across Rowena's face. "That's what I wish I could find out," she admitted. "Because some of them make no sense. Unless you believe they're my fault because a woman couldn't possibly manage a horse farm. That's what Cyrus thinks—'Horses are men's business.' I heard that when I became a jockey, and when I took courses in equine management at the university, and when I took over here. Oh, a woman doing exercising and mucking out the stable, that's okay. But as the *boss*?

Bad management, or bad luck. The stablehands are saying it too."

"Your stable staff adores you! They always have."

"That doesn't have anything to do with it. Since the fire, we've had four other incidents that could be blamed on my mismanagement. Or, according to superstition, on my owning the place at all! We had a valuable two-year-old here for training. Somehow a rope got tangled around his foreleg as he was running in the exercise barn—the leg broke, and he had to be put down. Another stallion being boarded here was permanently lamed as a result of carelessness. Whose, I haven't been able to find out. This year we've had a run of illnesses—viruses or bacteria; the laboratory still hasn't pinned it down. Two of my mares, and two sent here for breeding, have been barren . . . I had Dancer mated to Secretariat last spring," Rowena said, her eyes bright with tears. "She was in foal. I thought that proved we couldn't be having a recurrence of that disease that prevents conception . . . and a foal by Secretariat out of Bright Dancer would have been worth a fortune. It would have revitalized Unicorn Farm's breeding stock. And now . . ."

Now Dancer, and the future foal, were dead.

"I paid a fortune to mate Dancer to Secretariat," Rowena said in a voice that strove for hardness. "And I lost almost a hundred thousand in stud fees for those two mares last spring that didn't breed. I just paid every cent I have or could borrow for two fillies and two two-year-old stallions at the Saratoga sales, and I guess I'd better start praying that the curse on Unicorn Farm doesn't destroy them too. If that happens, I would have to sell. Or syndicate our stallions, which would make all past Drakes turn over in their graves."

I didn't exactly understand syndication, but that wasn't the explanation most needed now. "What's this garbage about a curse?" I demanded.

"Oh, that's a legend going back to the first settlers. A woman running Unicorn Farm is bad magic. Back during the French and Indian War a renegade Indian tried to attack the cabin while the settler was off with the fighting. His wife killed the Indian with his own tomahawk. In revenge, an Indian war party burned the whole settlement—after amusing themselves with the women and children first. And during the War Between the States, a Drake widow was running the breeding operations here. Nobody's too sure whether she was a Rebel or a Yankee; whichever she was, a raiding party from the other side tried to steal horses and there were a few more murders as a result. And back at the turn of the century there was some scandal or other at Derby time, between a Drake wife and somebody else's husband, that was also bad for Unicorn Farm business."

"Those stories are still going around? People believe them?" I was incredulous.

"Somebody at the *New York Times* dug them up at the time of the fire. A human interest story," Rowena said with some bitterness. "The Louisville paper picked it up. There's always a lot of superstitions around racetracks. I'm the first woman at the helm of Unicorn Farm since the scandal. Naturally, everybody's waiting to see how I work out. And some would prefer I don't."

"But who else would have taken it over?" I asked blankly. "You don't mean your uncle!"

"No. He had his chance when he was young, and he blew it. He also got in some kind of trouble while at college. I don't know what happened, but something obviously did. That's why my grandfather left Unicorn Farm to Dad, even though Uncle Ned was the elder son. And Uncle Ned's had . . . other troubles since."

She was referring to his drinking, I thought, and nodded.

"The last thing Ned really wants at this point is responsibility," Rowena said bluntly. "Oh, he likes strolling around offering guests mint juleps, and he'd love it if I depended on him for advice. But his advice is exactly what he'd do if he were the owner: sell Unicorn Farm, or at very least put Beauvais into syndication. Well, I won't. And that's the prime reason a lot of breeders around here think I don't know enough to run the place."

"You've been around horses and horse farms all your life! You've been a jockey, you almost won the Derby—"

"On a horse that had a mysterious accident. Don't forget that."

"Nobody ever said you caused it, did they? You've studied management, and breeding. You're *good* at what you do."

"Not good enough to prevent accidents or illness, apparently. Not good enough to keep owners coming here for boarding or for breeding, in spite of those things. Not that I can blame them. Look what happened to Dancer! I'm constantly braced against another casualty to Beauvais. If he couldn't stand at stud— As it is, I've had to dismiss several of the stable and maintenance staff as well as the housekeeper. Which hasn't exactly endeared me to my adoring stablehands!"

"But you'll manage," I said instinctively. "You just said you've borrowed enough to pay for the new stock. If you just do well with next winter's breeding—and Beauvais is still at stud, his foals bring high prices." Something struck me. "Rowena, I never thought! Should you be stuck with the expense of me right now?"

"Don't even start thinking that! Your mother had insurance. You're also entitled to social security payments till you're nineteen, and you've just inherited other assets. Enough to see you through college, and get you started. Besides, I'm not stuck with you. I want you. And I'm getting another stablehand and exercise girl, aren't I?" Rowena's voice was teasing, but her eyes were kind.

Outside in the darkness, something tapped lightly at the windowpanes. A faint spattering of rain, like ghostly fingers. But there were no real ghosts at Unicorn Farm; I knew it. If there had been, I would not have found it such a place of peace. There were only the ghosts of old superstitions, tragedies, and scandals. As for mysterious illnesses and accidents . . . maybe it was callous, but next to my mother's cancer, next to the horror of Rowena's parents' deaths by fire, they seemed as nothing. Unicorn Farm had been a sanctuary, a place of peace and hope. It would be again. I could help Rowena make it so.

All the rootlessness, the purposelessness, I'd felt since Mother's death crystallized into that firm resolve.

5

I awoke the next morning very early, so early that the sun was just flooding the horizon with streaks of gold. For a moment I lay in the strange bed, bewildered. Then everything began coming back.

Somewhere downstairs a door opened and slammed shut. Rowena, probably, going to the paddocks; her days started early. I slid out of bed and rummaged for jeans and a T-shirt in my partially unpacked suitcase. Dressed, I opened the bedroom door cautiously. The house was still, and from behind Dr. Drake's closed door came the sound of snoring. So he had come home sometime after Rowena and I had gone to bed.

I tiptoed downstairs and out the front door. Then I went down the broad steps of the porch, and all the remembered scents and sounds of the Kentucky dawn closed in on me. Birds were twittering; the air was alive with fragrance from the flower borders; the sky was gold and coral. All the old peace was back, and last night's apprehensions seemed very far away.

I followed the path around the house, past the side porch and the thrusting addition of the new kitchen. And there everything was, as I remembered it ... the acres of paddocks and the track, the miles of fences, the graveled paths and flower borders and allées of trees that led to the working part of Unicorn Farm. The business office that Uncle Gil had built near the manor house; the exercise pavilion; the farm manager's house. Behind it had been long, low wooden dormitories for farm workers; they were gone with the fire and had been replaced by temporary mobile housing units.

The stallion barn was new too—white trimmed with raspberry, the Unicorn Farm colors, but built of stucco-covered concrete blocks, not wood. The breeding barn was beyond it, and beyond that the familiar wooden barns for broodmares and their offspring. They were not there now, though; in summers, as Rowena had said, they stayed out in the soft night air.

Off to the left of the stallion barn I heard a well-remembered drawn-out whinny.

Beauvais. My heart lifting, I started running, and there he was, at the far end of his private paddock, rearing up on his hind legs as if he were a model for the rampant unicorn that was the symbol of Unicorn Farm.

"He's skittish today. Guess he figured out somebody special's coming." Cyrus appeared from the stallion barn, walking toward me with a bucket of Beauvais's favorite treat. *Oats and honey* ... Cyrus had let me feed Beauvais oats and honey when Dad brought me here that first time, shortly after Beauvais lost the Derby. I vaguely recalled that there had been talk about syndication then, only it had gone completely over my six-year-old head.

"Cyrus, what's syndication?" I asked abruptly.

Cyrus stopped short. "Who's been putting that idea in your head? Won't be none of that going on *here*. Miss Rowena's made up her mind, just like her dad. You best forget you ever heard tell of it." He chirruped loudly.

Across the field Beauvais became motionless. Then deliberately, playfully, he started toward us in a series of starts and stops. He put the brakes full on in the middle of the paddock, tossed his mane, and gazed at me sideways.

I whinnied.

An answering whinny came to me on the morning breeze, and then Beauvais came running. In another moment there he was, so *big*—I was always startled to realize his bigness—poking his dark muzzle into my neck, my arms, like a playful puppy. Looking for oats and honey, or for peppermints . . .

"He remembers," an amused voice said behind me. Rowena had come out of the stallion barn and was standing there with a reminiscent smile. A tall man stood behind her.

"Sarah, this is our neighbor, Gregory Stahl."

I blessed her for that *our*, making me a permanent part of Unicorn Farm, even as my eyes took in every detail of Rowena's boyfriend. He was in love with her, that was abundantly clear from the way he looked at her, even though Rowena'd carefully avoided admitting such a thing. His hair was bronzed gold, faintly curly, and his skin was bronzed too. His eyes were gray as ice. He wore what even I could tell were expensive European riding clothes—

chamois breeches and highly polished boots; a loden
jacket with silver buttons, and a riding hat. He carried a light leather whip beneath his arm, and he
bowed formally, though his voice, as he spoke to
me, was pleasant.

"Miss Burton, it's a pleasure. I've heard so much
about you from your cousin."

"Gregory just rode over to give Maximilian a
morning gallop," Rowena said, indicating a magnificent black stallion quietly munching hay by the
stallion barn.

No, he didn't, I thought involuntarily. Why, I
could not say. What I thought his objective had
been I could not say either. His face was impassive.
Then Beauvais butted my neck impatiently and licked
my ear, and we all laughed.

"I'm riding over to Haseley Hall to look at Greg's
new stud data from Austria," Rowena said. "Don't
you want to come? It will give you a chance to see
Greg's horses exercising." That's what she *said;*
what I heard was that she wanted company. I wondered why, but didn't ask. I just said, "Sure, what do
I ride on?" Rowena laughed and said she was sure
Cyrus could come up with an exercise pony that
would put up with me.

Within fifteen minutes we were galloping down
the grass strips, twenty feet wide, that separated
the stallion pastures. I was on Jeeter, a good-natured
Appaloosa; Rowena was on her favorite mare, Shining Star. It was unusual in Kentucky to see prize-
winning thoroughbreds used for riding; they were
far too valuable as breeding stock to risk their
having accidents. But Rowena, for all her tradition-
alism about Unicorn Farm, was a rebel too. She'd
been a jockey, so she was a careful rider, and she

felt it was unfair to keep horses who loved to run from doing so just because owners wanted to make money out of them. Greg was in the lead, but after a short while he paused and looked back, and I heard Rowena chuckle. In another minute she had dug her heels into Shining Star's rounded sides and was tearing down the strip of grass, passing Greg and Maximilian with a triumphant wave. I laughed.

Greg waited for me to catch up with him, and he laughed too. "Your cousin's quite a woman. Always unpredictable. Who else would be so stubborn about doing everything the old way, and then race on a mare that's in foal to Beauvais? Look at her!"

Rowena had jumped the fence dividing Unicorn Farm from Haseley Hall and was now sitting demurely, waiting with a look of mischief on her face.

"Maybe you can talk some sense in her," Greg said to me. Afterward, I was to kick myself for not asking what he meant. At that moment, all I was conscious of was an overwhelming sense of his presence, and of power. And of an inexplicable desire to get away from both. I pressed my heels into Jeeter and chirruped, and we took off at a reasonably fast rate of speed to join Rowena.

Greg joined us, and we cantered up a rise, and I had my first look at Haseley Hill in its new transformation. And everything else fled from my mind.

Gregory Stahl had poured a lot of money into it, Rowena had said. That was an understatement. Here were no creosoted fences, but miles of white rails that would receive expensive repainting every few years. The old stone mansion of my vague memories remained, but almost everything else was new. Stallion barns, breeding barn, barns for mares and foals, exercise facilities, offices—everything in slate-roofed white stucco, with dark crossbeams that gave them a faint flavor of the Austrian Tyrol. Greg even showed me a white Lippizaner in the stallion herd. The horse nuzzled me gently and rolled soft dark eyes.

"You may practice dressage on him sometimes if you wish," Greg told me courteously.

"I'd love to."

"Perhaps you will ride with your cousin in the horse show I hope to organize this October."

Rowena made no comment. Greg took her arm. "We're going to the business office to consult the computer," he said to me. "I'm sure you would like a chance to—what do you Americans say? 'Poke around' the Haseley Hall facilities. We're very proud of what we've done here," he added with a smile that went a long way toward explaining why Rowena put up with his imperious manner. "We hope to win architectural awards, as Gainesway Farm has done. Please go anywhere you like, and ask my staff any questions that you wish. And then feel free to join us."

He marched Rowena off toward the office before either of us could protest.

I left Jeeter tied to a convenient fence and wandered around the grounds. The Haseley Hall stock— gamboling in pastures, breakfasting quietly, exercising on the track—was, like Maximilian, magnificent. The Haseley Hall outbuildings reminded me of a luxury hotel. Everything sparkled—the white paint, the floors, the inside walls of imported woods with their high varnish. The elaborate wrought-iron gates, fit for a castle, on each horse stall. The brass nameplates by each doorway, giving the horse's name and the prizes he had won. The shiny vermilion-red buckets and brushes, each bearing its user's name. The tack at Unicorn Farm seemed very shabby by comparison.

A golden retriever ambled out of a stall and came to greet me, his tail a waving plume. I was scratching behind his ears, when a slim figure came walking purposefully through the barn's wide doorway. The sun was bright now, so the figure showed in silhouette. It stopped.

"What are you doing here?" Tim's voice demanded curtly.

"I could ask you the same thing," I replied with spirit. "I thought you worked next door!"

"Cyrus sent me over for something. I'm going back now. Want to come?"

I shook my head. "Not yet." For goodness' sake, I thought with confusion, why didn't I just say I was here with Rowena? What I did say was, "Thank you for the casserole last night. It was very good."

"Any time," Tim said. His mood had lifted. "Come eat with us hired hands at the bunkhouse some night."

"Hired hand yourself," I said promptly. "I intend to earn my board and keep around here. And I accept the invitation. Just tell me when."

"I'll do that," Tim said, and went out whistling. And I went, feeling my face warm, over to the office to join Rowena.

A secretary in a formal business suit told me Mr. Stahl and Miss Drake were in Mr. Stahl's private office and to go right in, because I was expected.

They didn't hear me enter.

They didn't hear because the computer on a side desk was whirring, but more because they were in the middle of an argument. That came through loud and clear despite their calm, low voices. ". . . the stubbornest woman it has ever been my good fortune to know," Greg was saying.

"Don't patronize me," Rowena snapped. "I'm a good horse breeder, and a better businesswoman than you're willing to admit."

"I do admit it. That is why I call you stubborn and not stupid. You should sell me Tapestry. You know it, and I know it, even your uncle knows it."

"Leave Ned out of this. He has nothing to say about the management of Unicorn Farm."

"I know that too. I am merely pointing out that the function of a stallion farm in the modern world is to sell stallions. You should sell Tapestry; it is the most sensible thing for you to do, both financially and for the sake of the Unicorn Farm bloodlines. You need new bloodstock. And do not tell me about your Saratoga purchases; they are insufficient and we both know it." His voice changed. "*Liebchen,* if you are determined to hold on to Tapestry, at least sell me a share. That would solve—"

"I told you I would not discuss that," Rowena interrupted sharply. Then she got her voice under control. "You can use Tapestry at stud, you know that. We could mate him with your Scheherezade; she's had good results and has excellent bloodlines. A foal of theirs should be profitable—and beautiful."

"Beautiful, yes." Greg went to the computer and keyboarded rapidly. Then he shook his head. "If you'll look at her lineage on the paternal side, and Tapestry's dam..." He went into a technical discussion I didn't understand. Rowena looked at the computer screen and frowned. Then Greg chuckled slightly. "Do not despair. We will book your Tapestry for a rendezvous with my Delilah. Their offspring may not be so *beautiful*, as you put it, but should have excellent speed and conformation."

I wondered fleetingly if Gregory Stahl was as cold-blooded about his own romances. But he couldn't be courting Rowena for her fortune, not after what she'd told me last night! Greg started keyboarding again, probably working out the stud arrangement he'd just suggested, and I knocked on the doorframe and announced my presence.

Rowena looked as if she was glad to see me. Greg invited us both out for dinner and she accepted. We went back outside, remounted, and rode home, and that was that. Except that as we rode I told Rowena about Tim's invitation for a bunkhouse dinner, and she looked puzzled.

"What was Tim Payne doing at Haseley Hall?"

"He said Cyrus sent him there for something."

Rowena nodded. I would have thought no more of it, but when we reached our own exercise track, Cyrus was standing by the fence, watching a two-year-old go through his paces. And Rowena asked him the same question. Cyrus's face was blank.

"I didn't send the young feller nowhere! Why'd he say that?"

"Never mind," Rowena said soothingly. "Sarah must have misunderstood." The heel of her riding boot came down on my toe.

"He's over eighty, and he's forgetful. He should have been retired years ago, except that I don't have the heart to do it to him," she murmured to me as we walked back to the house for a belated breakfast.

And that, as I said, was that.

Except that I didn't believe that in this instance Cyrus was forgetful.

*T*he rest of that August passed in a rose-colored daze. I was aware of all the problems on the farm, but distantly, the way you're conscious of a pinch given you through the sleeve of a heavy coat. The rose-gold glow was back on Unicorn Farm again, and it was working its old magic on me.

Through the rest of that golden August I rode Jeeter, mucked out stables, and curried broodmares and, occasionally, stallions when their grooms would let me. I exercised horses, too, at first under the stallion manager's critical supervision. He *was* critical, and he made me nervous.

"Don't let it get you," Tim advised when I admitted this in strictest confidence a week after my arrival, on the night I was his guest at the bunkhouse dinner table. I felt uncomfortable at first, and not just because I was the boss's cousin. The only person at the table whom I knew at all well, aside from Tim, was Cyrus. There was one woman, a pretty, brisk young brunette. The rest were men of assorted ages and jobs, who nodded when introduced and went on with technical horse talk that was mostly over my head. After the highly spiced beef and chicken stew known as burgoo, Tim announced we were taking our apple pie and iced tea into his "place." Nobody raised an eyebrow.

Tim's place was much like I imagined a college dorm room—small and cheerful. There were blown-up photographs of racing scenes on the walls. A Navajo blanket and huge pillows of Indian cotton converted the bed into a sofa. Pretty soon I was curled up on it while Tim sprawled comfortably in the canvas sling chair with his feet propped on the footboard.

After a while I felt so at ease I heard myself confessing my inferiority complex where the stallion manager was concerned.

"Beech treats everybody that way at first. And keeps doing it most of the time afterward, so get used to it," Tim added, grinning.

I grinned back, relieved. "I was afraid it was because I'm such a greenhorn. Or because I'm a girl."

"You think he'd dare act that way with his boss a woman?"

"Oh, come on. I know what most of the guys around here think of that idea, remember? Probably the very ones I just had dinner with."

Tim moved to the bed to slide an arm around my shoulders and give me a squeeze. "I admit some of them are kind of crude. But they're not bad once you get to know them. And they respect people strictly on the basis of horsemanship, not age, sex, or job description. You'd better believe Rowena gets respect, regardless of superstition. So does K. T. Healy."

"Was that the girl at dinner just now?"

Tim chuckled. "Don't call her a girl, or she may belt you. K.T.'s a licensed equine physical therapist. She works at Unicorn Farm only part-time, but she often stays for dinner when she does. Who else don't you know yet?"

I spread my hands helplessly. "Hardly anybody! I know Mr. Beech is the stallion manager. And I've met Helen Gallagher." She was Rowena's part-time secretary, a pleasant red-haired young woman who also kept the books.

"Big Joe Crawley's the maintenance chief. He was the one with the plaid shirt and the cigar. He's in charge of buildings, grounds, and gardens. He's got a small crew. So does Mr. Luckenbill—he's the farm manager. He lives in that stone house near the back drive, and he's responsible for all the crops raised at Unicorn Farm."

Tim went on to describe for me all the rest—the grooms and stablehands and exercisers, the chief trainer and his assistants.

"I'll never keep them straight!" I said ruefully.

"Sure you will. You remembered who I was, didn't you?" Tim teased. "Then there's what Rowena calls her 'consulting professionals,'" he went on. One by one, he took me through the list, with thumbnail descriptions and photographs in Unicorn Farm brochures: Mr. Gates, the farm's official treasurer and accountant. Dr. Voelkner, the vet, keen-eyed and shrewd. The lab technician at the university's school of veterinary medicine, whom Rowena occasionally consulted. The advertising and public relations firm that handled Unicorn Farm's stud and sales brochures. "And let's not forget Unicorn Farm's consulting geneticist and bloodlines expert," Tim added dryly. That was Dr. Drake's official title in the brochures.

When I went back to the main house it was very late, and though most of the names and job descriptions were still a jumble, I knew two things very well. There was, very definitely, good chemistry between Tim and me—though I wasn't sure where that would lead. And Unicorn Farm was, very definitely, a *business*.

I realized that more and more with each day that passed. Stallion breeding, training, and racing was *very* big business. I saw that every time I was around Haseley Hall, or around Greg Stahl, which was fairly often. Greg invited me over to Haseley Hall to ride or just hang around, partly because he knew it pleased me, partly because he knew it pleased Rowena.

I rode with either or both of them; I rode alone; I rode with Tim. I even, finally, got to exercise some of Unicorn Farm's stallions on my own. My body stopped feeling stiff and achy, and got used to being in the saddle. I had dinner with Tim again—not at the bunkhouse, but at a cheerful, inexpensive restaurant he liked downtown. I went to the movies with Tim, and over to the racetrack, where he showed me around. Greg also took me to dinner with him and Rowena—at the country club, at the Mansion restaurant, at Demos' Coach House. He took Rowena out by herself frequently, and she didn't always tell me where.

All at once it was Labor Day, and I didn't know one bit more about my future. I'd been living, I admitted to myself, in an escapist vacuum.

"School must be starting!" Rowena said, startled, as we were having breakfast on the side porch on Labor Day. "I'd better act like a guardian and call about that tomorrow. And shouldn't we be buying you some new fall clothes? The winter weather's quite different here from what you're used to in Connecticut. Don't worry about the money. I got a check from your mother's bank yesterday."

"I wish I didn't have to go back to high school!" I exclaimed abruptly. The thought of doing senior year in a new school, with strangers, was unnerving. I hadn't even finished the last weeks of my junior year, because I'd stayed home to be with Mother. My guidance counselor had arranged for me to study on my own and take final exams with her as monitor. With all that had happened, I didn't feel like a high school student anymore.

Rowena was looking at me closely. "What would you *want* to do?" she asked me.

"I don't know.... Just stay here and work with horses, really. Till I get my head straight."

"Don't you want to go to college?"

"Probably, but not right away. I don't even know what I want to do with my life—at least, anything sensible!"

"Suppose you didn't have to be sensible?"

I grinned. "Work with horses, like you do. Except that I wasn't lucky enough to inherit a horse farm, and I've learned enough to know either you're born to it, or you need a lot of money—that is, if you want to make a decent living. I wouldn't want to be somebody else's stablehand forever. I guess that means I'm stuck with finishing high school even if I dread it."

"Maybe not," Rowena said thoughtfully. And that was all she would say on the subject.

There are no such things as days off when you

work with animals. Labor Day meant the same daily labor. Rowena was closeted in the study, examining the August bookkeeping records. The sky was an uneasy yellow-gray, and there was static in the still air. Shadow, the black setter that was Beauvais's stablemate, felt it; he paced restlessly back and forth and whined.

Beauvais, on his way in from the fields to his stall, gave an answering whinny. Then he reared, almost jerking his lead from Cyrus's hands.

"Whoa, boy! Easy!" Cyrus saw me and beckoned with a jerk of his head. "The boy's mad at me a-cause it's going to storm. He always hates storms. Mebbe he'll mind his manners for you a-cause you're a lady." He offered me the lead and I took it, knowing this was a high compliment.

Beauvais nuzzled me to search for peppermints, and I pulled away, laughing. "Not now, you rascal! Maybe after you're inside, if you behave!"

Beauvais blinked his long lashes at me and went with me docilely, though I could feel him trembling. Inside the stall, Shadow performed his circling maneuver of battening down straw to lie on, and Beauvais stuck out a pink tongue as a signal he wanted his reward. I put the candy on it, and he flipped it a couple of times, savoring the pungent mint before chomping.

"You have that beast eating out of your hand, don't you?" Dr. Drake was leaning against the wrought-iron gate, pleased with his pun.

"He's not a beast, he's a beauty," I said neatly. I came out, latching the gate behind me. From the next stall Beau's son Tapestry whinnied a request for peppermints too. I obliged, scratching his forehead. Then I started out of the barn. The doctor followed.

"All the same, Beau's as crazy about you as he is about Rowena." He looked me up and down with a kind of significance that made me uncomfortable. "Too bad you can't own a piece of him."

"He's a hundred percent Rowena's, and she'll never have it any other way," I said flatly.

"More's the pity. Rowena prides herself on being a liberated woman, but where Unicorn Farm's concerned, she's as old-fashioned as her father was." Dr. Drake fumbled with his pipe.

"I thought Cyrus didn't allow smoke around Beauvais."

"That old goat should have been retired long ago," Dr. Drake retorted, looking like an overweight goat himself. He sent up a cloud of smoke, and Beauvais snorted. "If you really want to earn your keep around here, young lady, you'll persuade Rowena to bring this place into the twentieth century. Gregory Stahl has the right idea, but of course she won't listen to him either. About syndication, or about anything else!"

"All I know about syndication is that Rowena doesn't believe in it."

"Oh, she believes in it, all right, but not for Unicorn Farm!" To my dismay, Dr. Drake settled himself purposefully on the bench outside Beau's stall. "Syndication, Miss Innocence, means the owner of a valuable piece of horseflesh like the one in there hedges his bets by sharing the wealth and sharing the risks. The original owner of the horse gets to have hundreds of thousands or more dollars worth of his assets in cash rather than on the hoof."

"I don't understand," I said encouragingly. If I

was going to be stuck in conversation with Rowena's uncle, I might as well learn something in the process.

Dr. Drake regarded me under beetling brows. "You understand cash on hand, don't you? If my niece could talk herself into dividing the ownership of Unicorn Farm's main asset, there, into twenty to forty shares, she could keep a block of those shares herself and sell the others to investors for several grand apiece. Each owner would get to breed one mare per share to Beauvais each year, for a fee, and would get a percentage of what Beau earned in stud fees from outsiders. Less the cost of maintaining him in style, of course. Rowena'd get this place out of the red, and we'd all make money."

"I thought you didn't own any of Unicorn Farm," I let out involuntarily. Dr. Drake shot me an acid glance.

"So you're not as ignorant as you pretend. No, my dear, I do not. My esteemed father took care of that, with a little help from myself. But as you certainly have also noticed, I am a consultant and wage-slave around the old Kentucky home. In other words, when Unicorn Farm prospers, I prosper. When it does not, I don't."

"Dr. Drake, K.T. just took Tapestry in for therapy and she'd like you to take a look at his right foreleg while he's in the pool," Tim said coldly from behind me.

The doctor heaved himself from the bench amid a cloud of smoke. "Therapy, schmerapy! The girl's a glorified swimming teacher! In my day, horses swam by instinct."

"Yes, and were put down if their legs went bad." Tim's thrust meant nothing to me, but it seemed to mean something to the doctor. His always red complexion darkened and he took himself off, lurching a little.

Tim looked after him. "Has he been drinking?"

At his censorious tone my mood, which had been one of relief, did a reversal. "He always walks that way, and you know it. Do you always have to suspect the worst?"

"Only when I'm afraid I'm going to find it." Tim grinned. "Lighten up, will you? I really wasn't trying to pick a fight. But he gets me mad when he acts like such a know-it-all." He looked at me. "Was that creep coming on to you? Don't laugh, I mean it. If he gives you problems, you tell me, understand?"

"And you can do something about it, I suppose?"

"Yes, I can."

Tim said it quietly, but there was so much certainty, so much—authority, in the three words, I was startled. It must have showed. Tim looked sheepish, and grinned again. "Sorry, I didn't mean to come on strong, either."

I did laugh, then, my tension easing. "Whatever Dr. Drake is, the one thing I'm sure he isn't is a dirty old man. Actually, he was giving me a sales pitch—for me to give Rowena."

"Don't tell me. Syndication, right? Or has he progressed to advising her to sell Unicorn Farm? Or is he seeing curses all over the place?"

"Don't joke about that," I said.

"Forget it. I didn't mean to. Actually, I came here to ask you if you'd like to go downtown to a movie tonight. I'll see anything but a slasher story."

For some reason, a shudder ran down my spine.

"I'd like that," I said after a moment. "Only promise me it won't be anything about horse farm big business, or mad doctors, or anything that's creepy!"

"We'll find something nice and soothing," Tim promised, looking happy. "Something totally G-rated. Or we could probably watch an old movie on Rowena's VCR. She wouldn't mind. She's going out someplace with the Rich Swiss."

That was his nickname for Gregory Stahl.

"I'd better go see if K.T. or Mr. Beech have any work for me," I said hastily. "One of Rowena's video movies would be fine."

"Better stay away from K.T. if you don't want to bump into Dr. Drake," Tim advised. "I'll catch up with you later to arrange about tonight."

I didn't report to the stallion manager, because when I spotted him he was in the middle—or rather, on the receiving end—of a loud fight with Dr. Drake. I heard the gist of it from K.T. when I joined her.

"Doc has decided Tapestry's lameness is the result of deliberate sabotage on Beech's part." K.T.'s eyes sparked with irritation. She was young—she'd completed the university's equine therapy graduate program only a few years ago—and I liked her. "You'd better tell Miss D to put a muzzle on the old coot. Beech has been remarkably patient, but he's had about all of Doc that he can take. Another blowup and he may quit. He's had plenty of offers to work elsewhere at higher pay."

"You mean Dr. Drake's been going around accusing the stallion manager of—of—!"

"You got it, sweetie," K.T. said.

I spent the rest of the day helping K.T. steer horses through the swimming pool and the horse Jacuzzi. And wondering exactly what, and how, to report to Rowena. And eventually, washing down some skittish yearlings after their training sessions. We were still due for an electric storm and they were restless. One of the yearlings succeeded in knocking his full bucket out of my hands. Water and yellow dust from the dry earth spattered over me.

I went back to the manor house to make repairs, and met Rowena. She was dressed in cool white chiffon, and she looked me up and down and laughed.

"I wish I had a picture of you like that! Go take a shower. Greg's picking me up in half an hour to attend a small dance at the country club, and he's invited you to come along."

"I have a date with Tim."

"Tim can come too. If he can clean the mud off. I caught a glimpse of him out the back window a while ago. You can call him on the house phone; if he's not back at the dorm yet, try the other buildings."

So I did, and Tim said okay, he'd be happy to go.

It was a magical night. That was what I was to remember afterward, the candlelight and flowers on the table, the look in Gregory Stahl's eyes as he danced with Rowena, and the radiance on her face. For this night, at least, she was forgetting about the problems plaguing Unicorn Farm. I could tell Greg wasn't raising the touchy subject of syndication. What he *was* saying to her I didn't know, because I was listening to Tim.

Afterward, I couldn't have told you what Tim and I talked of, either. It ranged from horse training, to Tim's university classes, to the movie we had seen last week. What I was really aware of was the admiration in Tim's eyes when he first saw me in my apricot-colored dress, and the shock I'd felt when his eyes met mine.

I hadn't seen Tim dressed up until that night, when Greg pulled up in the Mercedes and Tim came swinging toward us from the bunkhouse as a crack of heat lightning split the sky. He was wearing a dark blue suit with a wine-colored tie.

Tim wasn't handsome, but he was interesting-looking, with the olive-gold skin that came from being so much outdoors, and that brown-gold hair and unusual gray-brown eyes. In the light from the candles on the dinner table, they were almost golden. All that seemed to matter that night was the interest and intimacy growing between us, not mere words. Maybe that was why certain words didn't register more strongly.

The four of us sat a dance out together on the veranda after dinner. The storm still hadn't struck, but an odd wind had risen. It riffled my hair and the hem of my apricot dress. Tim was leaning toward me, teasing me, and the expression in his eyes was champagne to my soul. I was glad that I'd taken trouble with my hair, that I'd worn the dress that was one of the last things Mother'd helped me buy. I was thinking of that, but I wasn't choking up. What was real was the way Tim looked at me, and the way we fit together on the dance floor, and my feeling glad about that and about looking grown-up and good.

I felt even more grown-up when two distinguished-looking couples paused beside us. Gregory rose, and so did Tim, and there was a flurry of introductions. One couple was from Lexington, and known to both Greg and Rowena. The other two were friends of Greg's. He introduced us formally: "Mr. and Mrs. Patrick Bellington of West Palm Beach, Florida. We met at the races there two years ago.

Miss Rowena Drake, and her cousin, Miss Sarah Burton, of Unicorn Farm. And Mr. Timothy Payne, who is also associated with Unicorn."

There was a delighted little flutter of recognition, for the Bellingtons had seen Rowena race on Beauvais. Then Mr. Bellington looked at Tim, squinting.

"But I know you, too, don't I? Not from Kentucky. The name isn't familiar, but I'm sure we've met. On the Florida racing circuit somewhere."

Tim shook his head politely. "Mr. Stahl flattered me when he introduced me. I'm not part of the racing world yet—I'm a college student from Upstate New York, and I work for Miss Drake part-time. I only wish I could afford the Florida horse scene!"

At that moment the storm broke in a clap of thunder and a torrent of driving rain. There was a concerted rush for the clubhouse door. Inside, the orchestra was playing something we both liked. Tim's arm went around me and he swept me out onto the floor. We fit together as if made for each other.

We fit together even better, and closer, when we were back at the manor house later. The rain stopped just as Greg pulled up at the front steps. He and Rowena went straight inside. Tim turned to me.

"Feel like taking a walk?"

I nodded wordlessly. The air was very fresh, and cool, and we walked hand in hand over the wet grass. Not very far; just to the concealing umbrella of the weeping cherry tree. Then Tim took me in his arms.

It was the first time Tim kissed me. The first time, I'll be honest, that I'd been *really* kissed, and really kissed back. I hadn't had much experience before Mother's illness had suddenly made dating and boys the last things on my mind. When Tim released me, and we stood for a moment staring at each other, I thought dizzily that I was a fast learner, or Tim a very good teacher, or both. Then I realized that Tim was almost as shaken as I was myself.

He kissed me again, but lightly, and disappeared into the darkness in the direction of the bunkhouse. I went like a sleepwalker into the manor house and up to bed, conscious only of the feel of Tim's mouth on mine.

CHAPTER

7

I woke much later than usual the next morning, with the memory of Tim's kiss still vivid in my mind. Then I dragged myself to the shower, half expecting to see some change in my reflection as I passed the mirror. I looked a little spaced out, but that was all. Which was probably just as well.

I was still dressing when the telephone rang. It was Rowena, on the house phone, summoning me to her office. She greeted me with an enigmatic smile. "You don't have to go back to high school if you don't want to. I've been talking to your guidance counselor back in Connecticut, and to the school administration here. How would you like to stay home from school this year, Sarah, and take part-time courses at the university here instead?"

First I goggled at her. Then I let out a yell and hugged her.

"But is that possible?" I asked when I got my breath. Rowena nodded.

"A lot of colleges now will let highly motivated high school students go directly into college without a secondary school diploma. If they've completed the required courses and credits in their home state, and if their grades are good enough. You have, and yours are. Your counselor's sending your transcripts down by overnight mail, and you can start at the university by taking nine credits worth of courses this fall as a part-time student. You'll have to take SATs sometime this fall. In the spring, or next fall if you prefer, you can begin attending college full-time. Later, if you'd rather, you can transfer to another college somewhere else."

Right now, taking a few college courses in Lexington and spending all the rest of my time at Unicorn Farm was my idea of bliss.

After that, things moved quickly. The transcripts came. I had an interview at the university and, with Tim's help, pored over the catalog for course offerings. Rowena and I, in our spare time, went clothes shopping. I opened a bank account. And with no more ado than that, I became a college student.

Though I didn't admit it, I was a little scared that I'd feel out of place. But I didn't. I'd changed even more in the past year than I'd known. And Tim's friendship helped me feel like a real college student. I was taking nine credits—Survey of World Literature, Introduction to Psychology, and a biology course I could have lived without—to Tim's seventeen. But he usually managed to be around with the farm's van or his own battered Honda, whenever I was ready to go home. He took me to a couple of movies on campus, and he helped me study for the SATs, which were coming up in October.

The rest of the time—*most* of the time—both of us worked. In the stables. With the stallions—I was being allowed to exercise some of the stallions now.

"You're coming along," K.T. approved, leaning on the fence to watch me early one morning. "I have to admit, when Miss D said she was bringing in a kid with no training, just because she was a relative, I was worried. Most people who work with horses have done it all their lives. But you've done okay."

"Tim didn't grow up with horses either, did he?"

"Oh, he's worked around them a lot, all right," K.T. said dryly. "Where, I couldn't say. Regular mystery man as far as biographical details are concerned. Not that that's unusual around horse barns, or that it matters. Not if the person's work is good, and his is."

"How did he get here, anyway?" I asked in what I hoped was a casual manner. K.T. shot me a quizzical glance.

"He showed up one afternoon last February, in the middle of foaling season. Said he was a university student needing a job and he'd heard around the pre-vet program that Miss D needed help. Did she ever! Unicorn Farm was having a streak of unexplained fevers running through the breeding stock, and a couple of new foals had died. Dr. Drake had accused the stablehands of not keeping the stables warm enough, and two of them had quit. Miss D had already interviewed a few people, but even though she was desperate, she'd held off on hiring somebody. But she liked Tim and she took him on."

"He's never . . . said anything about being part of the Florida horse scene, has he?"

"He's never said much of anything about himself. Like I said, mystery man." K.T. grinned. "I thought maybe *you'd* have gotten more out of him." I blushed.

Tim did know about horses, and he clearly loved them. He cut classes to be at Unicorn Farm when Rowena's Saratoga purchases arrived. Two fillies and two two-year-old stallions—they were soft-eyed, mischievously capricious and enchanting. Greg rode over on Maximilian at dawn the next day to take a look, and was impressed enough to urge Rowena to groom the stallions for the Wood Memorial race for three-year-olds next April—like all thoroughbreds, these two would have their official birthdays on January first. Rowena, Mr. Beech, and Mr. Gilfillan, the trainer, held long conferences, debating the potential of all the Unicorn Farm stock. To my delight, I was allowed to help exercise the new acquisitions.

September turned into October, and both Rowena's and my social life suffered. I had the SATs to take. Greg was deeply involved in big business deals and in preparations for his Haseley Hall Invitational Horse Show. One of the international companies on whose boards he sat was presenting a silver cup. I gathered the horse show had a mixed bag of business and social motives, but the proceeds were going to a local charity; Greg's own company was underwriting the event.

"And you must definitely compete, representing Unicorn Farm," he told Rowena persuasively.

"My jumper died, remember?" Rowena said briefly.

"I would consider it an honor to loan you one," Greg said firmly.

Rowena did not say no, as he clearly would have

refused to hear it, but the next morning found her taking Tapestry over jumps.

"Is he over his lameness?" I asked her apprehensively.

"K.T. says he's in fine condition now, and Beech and Gilfillan both agree. Tapestry loves jumping and tight squeezes; I remember that from when he was a two-year-old!"

Secretly I thought that considering Unicorn Farm's current state, it was foolhardy of Rowena to risk a member of her valuable stud stock.

Greg Stahl had no financial considerations to hamper him, and he was spending money as though it grew like bluegrass, getting ready for what the stable crew ironically referred to as his party. He was actually having a regulation show-jumping course laid out at Haseley Hall. Lexingtonians, who remembered when jumping contests were spontaneous affairs conducted (under influence of mint juleps) over rail fences and brambles and creeks and ditches, snickered. But they bought tickets anyway, and paid huge sums to enter as contestants.

Four days before the horse show, Tim rang the door bell of the manor house in the late afternoon. "Where's Rowena?" he demanded. When I said in the study, he opened the study door and marched in without knocking.

"I think you'd better come out to the stallion paddocks. Tapestry's favoring that leg again."

Rowena looked up, startled. "He was fine during practice this morning!"

"He's not fine now."

I tagged along as they strode out back. Tim was right.

Rowena, frowning, summoned K.T., Gilfillan, Tom

Beech, and Dr. Voelkner. I don't know what took place between them, but the next morning Tapestry was back in water therapy, and when I came home from my psych class, Rowena was nowhere to be seen. Cyrus, his face ominous, told me that she was "out back."

His gesture took in the whole hundred acres. I rode out on Jeeter, feeling apprehensive.

Rowena, in full horse-show dress, was taking Beauvais over hurdles.

The picture they made, dark horse and dark-clad rider moving as one into the autumn air, was so beautiful that for a moment I just sat back and marveled. Then, as soon as all four hooves were firmly on the ground, I let out a shout.

"Are you out of your cotton-picking mind?"

"Cotton is one crop we don't grow at Unicorn Farm." Rowena and Beauvais cantered over, both looking enormously pleased with themselves. "Do you know the latest rumor making the rounds of Lexington?" she demanded. I could guess—that the curse on Unicorn Farm had struck again. "I have no intention," Rowena said, eyes sparking, "of having Unicorn Farm withdraw from that horse show."

"You could borrow the horse Greg calls three times a day to offer you."

"I do not intend to have Unicorn Farm patronized by Haseley Hall."

"Rowena, be serious! Greg can afford to risk a valuable horse better than you can."

"That is exactly why I don't intend to let him." Rowena's face softened. "You're thinking about Beauvais's weak leg, aren't you? Don't worry, Sarah. He wouldn't dare try a long race like the Derby, but a horse show's different. It's very short spurts, and dexterity, and precision. Beauvais is fine in all of those, and so am I. Mr. Beech even says that riding Beau in the horse show will be the best possible advertisement that Unicorn Farm's very much in business and Beau's at the top of his form."

I couldn't help it; a shiver ran down my spine.

Somebody else disapproved of Rowena's decision: Dr. Drake. I found this out in the most uncomfortable way—he buttonholed, not Rowena, but me.

"What is that niece of mine up to?" he demanded.

"You'd better ask Rowena that," I answered evasively.

"I'm asking you, and don't bother playing innocent with me. You seem to be the recipient of all Rowena's confidences these days, not I. Is she seriously contemplating taking that valuable horse over show jumps?"

"Ask her," I repeated, and fled.

I heard the resulting scene, because it took place in high decibels in the most prominent area of the barn complex. It was short and to the point. Rowena, in an icy calm, made the situation perfectly clear: she was the sole owner of Unicorn Farm, and she would ride Beauvais when and where she thought it was in Unicorn Farm's and Beauvais's best interest.

"You're crazy!" Dr. Drake shouted after a shocked pause.

"Then it runs in the family, doesn't it?" Rowena snapped. "I'm warning you; if I hear one more word out of you till after that cup's awarded, you can pack your bags and take off! I don't care where!"

"You needn't be concerned with that," Dr. Drake retorted, deeply offended. "I'll be on the plane for some racetrack where the company is more congenial. You won't see me until that stunt of Stahl's is over!"

He took himself off. Unfortunately it was by way of the stable, where he proceeded to accuse Gilfillan of deliberately mistreating the stallions. Mr. Gilfillan, pushed beyond his limit, quit.

Cyrus, of course, was torn between fear that the curse would strike again and pride in his beloved Beau and Miss Rowena. What the rest of the stable staff thought, I found out from Tim: They were placing bets.

"On whether Rowena will win, or whether the curse will strike?" I retorted.

"Both."

Dr. Drake departed one hour later. Just afterward, Greg swung rapidly into Unicorn Farm's back drive on his Mercedes. It was now early evening, so no one but Rowena and I were around. He braked sharply and climbed out to intercept us as we were walking in some discouragement toward the manor house.

"What's going on around here? The news is all over the country club that Gilfillan just accepted a new job." He named a horse farm more famous, and considerably larger, than Unicorn Farm. "Why on earth did you let him go?"

"It certainly didn't take you long to find out about it," Rowena said tartly.

"I was at the country club. I can guarantee you every member knows by now, or will within the next half hour. I have absolute respect for you as a horsewoman, but if you intend to make a success of horse breeding as a business, you must learn to retain control of every aspect of the operation."

"I can scarcely force an employee to stay when he wants to leave," Rowena retorted, nettled.

"*I* could. Anyway, it is well known Gilfillan did not want to leave. He was driven to it by your uncle's irresponsible talk. What was the issue this time, anyway? It could not have been important enough for you to allow a valuable staff member to transfer allegiance to a competitor."

"I'm really not sure," Rowena said carelessly. I must have gasped, for the heel of her riding boot came down hard upon my toe. Then she drew herself up in what Uncle Gil used to call her "ruling monarch air." "Really, Greg. Here in Kentucky, we don't regard our fellow horse breeders as competitors, except on the racecourse!"

"Then you are too soft-hearted, or perhaps soft-headed, to make Unicorn Farm a successful business," Greg said bluntly. "You had much better sell it to me before you let its reputation all slip away." As Rowena's eyes shot fire, he smiled disarmingly. "This is not the time or place for a discussion of that, I know. You know my offers—*all* of them," he added with significance. "I will see what I can do about finding you another trainer. And you had better accept my offer of a mount. It will be important for everyone to see that Rowena Drake and Unicorn Farm are still winners."

"I don't know what I want to do about the horse show yet," Rowena answered vaguely. "And I can find my own trainer, thank you."

"What was that all about?" I demanded once Rowena had gotten rid of Greg and we were in the kitchen eating dinner.

Rowena grimaced. "He's right that it's important Unicorn Farm makes a good showing Saturday! The best way to do that is for no one but ourselves to know I'm entering it on Beau."

"You don't think the stablehands are going to keep quiet! They all know. They're betting on the results!"

"They'll keep quiet. One, because they'll get better betting odds if other bettors don't know Beau's involved. Two, because I've told them everyone working on the farm will get a sizable bonus *if* Beau's entrance Saturday is a big surprise. That's what's known as managing by incentive!"

I diplomatically avoided that touchy subject for a different one. "What *are* you going to do about replacing Gilfillan?"

"I don't know yet. Do the training myself, maybe."

"Now I *know* you're crazy!"

"I used to do it. I was good too." Rowena sighed. "Anyway, I won't think about it till after Saturday's over."

"Rowena, are you sure entering it on Beau is a good idea?" I hesitated. "All things considered?"

"You mean considering all the catastrophes we've had?" Rowena looked at me squarely. "Yes, I do. That's the real reason I'm doing it, and the reason I'm keeping it a secret. If Beau and I sail through safely, that should put a stop to superstition, if not to rumors. And if no one knows Beau's going to be entered, there'll be no chance for anyone to arrange another convenient natural disaster like the fire or broken limbs or viruses that have been staged already. Sarah, this spaghetti sauce is good. You'll have to write down the recipe for me."

"Forget the spaghetti!" I almost shouted. "Are you telling me you think that was deliberate sabotage?"

"You know I think that. We talked about it the

night you came, don't you remember?" Rowena went on dishing herself a second helping, so very calmly. "The very fact that those horses died of a virus or bacteria no one's ever heard of, that no other farm in Lexington's been infected with—I remember I hesitated about telling you all that when you'd just had so many troubles of your own. But I felt you had to know."

"I'm not talking about the horses' deaths! I'm talking about—" I forced my voice to sound natural. "I'm talking about the fire. You never said you suspected anything about the fire. Uncle Gil and Aunt Roberta died in that fire. That would be like—like if somebody had deliberately caused my mother to die of cancer." Rowena didn't speak, and when I went on, it was in a whisper. "Rowena, do you know what that means?"

"Oh, yes," Rowena said. "It means murder."

*S*he said it so absolutely calmly, as if she'd accepted the fact of her parents' murder long ago, that I, who had not shed a tear through or since my mother's terminal illness, looked and was stunned. Not at the word *murder*, but at her calm. And then it occurred to me that maybe calmness was the only way she'd been able to get through it; that she'd had more than enough to anesthetize her, and there were enough things she was actively worrying about already.

There was a time for everything, and two nights before a public appearance at which Rowena would need every bit of concentration she could summon was not the time to discuss the possible murder of her parents. I just nodded, and we finished the meal in silence.

I had a very solemn feeling as I went through my stable chores on Friday. Behind Cy's back I gave Beauvais an extra ration of his favorite oats and honey. He needed confidence too.

On Saturday we rose at an hour early even for a

horse farm. There was an autumn chill in the air; the grooms had put on another layer of sweaters, and steam rose from the stallions' nostrils as they stamped the straw. Horse show or no horse show, the regular early morning routines prevailed. Nobody talked much; whether through moroseness, superstition, or custom, I wasn't sure.

"You want Beau taken out or kept in?" Cy asked Rowena.

"Let him have his morning exercise," Rowena answered. "He deserves it! We'll drive the trailer out to his paddock when it's time." Although Haseley Hall adjoined Unicorn Farm, Beauvais would be transported there in style. With all the people and vehicles that would be milling around, this would be safer for him. It would also make his grand entrance more of a surprise.

Greg had arranged the horse show to take place in a series of eliminations, until ultimately the six riders who had covered the steeplechase jumps in the shortest time would compete against each other. The first heat was due to start in early afternoon, but Rowena told me spectators and participants would be arriving through the morning. By ten A.M., the sun was golden in a brilliant sky and the air had only a pleasant nip.

"Nice for tailgate picnics," Rowena commented.

At eleven she went in to dress. She emerged looking like a photograph out of *Town and Country* magazine, her hair sleeked into a chignon above an immaculate white neck stock, her off-white breeches and black riding coat tailored to perfection, her boots dazzling. It occurred to me that I, too, ought to help keep up Unicorn Farm's image, and Rowena hunted up some of her old riding clothes for me to wear.

It's a good thing riding styles don't change with time, I thought when I stared in the mirror. It was astonishing how much I looked like Rowena.

We went down to find that Cyrus and the stallion manager had already coaxed Beau into the trailer. Rowena herself would drive. I climbed in beside her, noting that Beau wasn't in the special trailer that bore his name, but in one carrying only the unicorn symbol and the lettering UNICORN FARM. He's traveling incognito, like a rock star, I thought, suppressing a slightly hysterical giggle.

Ironbridge Pike had a good deal of traffic today, and the ring road when we swung onto it had even more. Although our lands abutted, Haseley Hall's entrance was on the other road. The drive was clogged, and as we reached the open gates we found out why: Greg had men in full uniform checking everyone's identification and admission tickets. They wore guns.

I looked at Rowena in amazement. "Private *police?*"

"Security guards. Most of the larger farms around here have them."

"Why don't you, all things considered?" I asked. I knew about Unicorn Farm's sophisticated burglar alarm system and closed-circuit TV coverage of all gates, buildings, and stallion stalls. But they no longer seemed enough.

"Twenty-four-hour guards cost too much," Rowena said bluntly. Then she sighed. "If anything else fishy happens, I'll have to consider guards, despite the cost."

We parked in the shade in the area designated

for participants, and Rowena opened the trailer windows but didn't bring Beau out. "He's content in there; Shadow's with him. I'll wait till it's time for contestants to assemble at the entrance to the course."

We made the rounds of the tailgate parties, as was expected of us. Rowena smilingly parried questions about whom she was planning to hire as Unicorn's new trainer, about what horse she would be riding in the show. Greg was busy circulating, being a host, but as soon as he spotted Rowena, he detached himself from the people he was with and strode over.

"Rowena! As usual, you look magnificent."

"Thank you, Gregory. As usual, I must return the compliment." Rowena was right; he looked splendid in Austrian riding habit and medals, exuding power. She parried his questions also. "Just an old nag I dug up in the back lot," she quipped when he asked about her mount.

I had seen horse shows on TV, but not live, and it was every bit as exciting as I had imagined. Perhaps more; there was a precision, a sense of controlled power under the gentility, that was overwhelming.

Rowena was entered in the third heat, and sometime before that she slipped away so quietly I didn't even miss her till she was gone. It was around that time that Tim appeared beside me. "How did you get here?" I demanded. Ticket prices, I knew, were astronomical.

For answer, he flipped a badge pinned to his sweater. GROOM, UNICORN FARM, ENTRY #15, it said. "Cy sent me over. He thought Rowena should have a groom in attendance, and he didn't want to leave Tapestry. His fever's getting worse. Where *is* Rowena?"

"Off acting as her own groom somewhere."

The third heat was announced. The first two entries made more than respectable times. Then over the loudspeaker—trust Greg to have the full trappings of a professional announcer and speaker system—the next entry was announced.

"Number fifteen: Miss Rowena Drake, representing Unicorn Farm, on Beauvais."

There wasn't a loud noise. These people were too well-bred to shout. But all at once the air had become electric, and there was appreciative applause as Rowena rode onto the course, circling to inspect the jumps as each entrant was entitled to do. Then she lined up at the starting mark. For an instant she went still. Beauvais went still also, looking like one of his own publicity photographs, his ears alert, one forefoot slightly raised. Then Rowena gave an imperceptible signal, and they were off.

Rowena's actual final time was something like three minutes. But for me, from that moment she leaned slightly forward, as poised and motionless as a cat prepared to spring, time ceased. I was conscious, not of a clock ticking, but of the pounding of my heart.

Beau took the first jump, a replica of Lexington's familiar white fences, easily. Rowena swung him smartly to the left, lining up for the next, a wood barricade painted to look like a red and white barn door. Again that momentary pause, then they sailed over, horse and horsewoman as one. There was applause, like a wave breaking.

Next was the reproduction of an English hedgerow, which to my eyes looked more like an elongated haystack. Beau cleared it with inches to spare.

There was a flurry of whispers as Rowena wheeled Beau right for the next jump. It was deceptive, just another section of fence, but at an angle for which the jumper, coming right from the hedgerow, had to line up carefully. Precious seconds could be lost doing that. But if it wasn't done, the angle of jumping could be wrong. And the top rail or rails of the fence could be dislodged, resulting in a loss of points.

Beside me, Tim muttered, "She just lost four seconds." Again, ever so briefly, Rowena and Beau went still. Then he was in the air, clearing the hurdle.

A cry went up. Beau had cleared it, but his off rear hoof had grazed the top rail. It teetered. It regained balance and was still—on its proper support, not falling. The cry turned to applause. Rowena and Beau were flashing on, oblivious.

The next jump was positioned in the center of the ring, a high "brick" wall. I could see a muscle pulsing by Beau's eye as Rowena lined him up. My throat constricted. He was tiring . . . it didn't slow his speed, but he wasn't able to keep both back hooves high enough. One "brick" came crashing down. Penalty.

My heart was hurting, and I almost couldn't look. Two more obstacles—another fence, a series of rails like parallel bars—and then the water jump. I'd seen that ruin the timing of three other proud jumpers already. It was a diabolically clever obstacle, a "hedgerow" followed immediately by a small pond in which the horse had to land, only to scramble up quickly to jump out across another series of parallel bars. Greg was enormously proud of having copied the jump from a notorious one at the famous Badminton horse trials in England.

Beau was no spring chicken. Could he make it? Coward that I was, as he and Rowena flew into the air and over the "hedgerow," I buried my face in Tim's sleeve. Then came a roar of excitement, and Tim's laugh.

"You can look now. They made it!"

Beau sailed over the final fence rails, winning the heat with five seconds to spare.

In the next heat, someone bettered Rowena's time by thirty seconds. Then, in the first round of eliminations, Beau had trouble with that one top rail again. He cleared it, barely, but he was no sooner over than the top rail fell. He did lose points. Fortunately, a few other horses lost points also during this heat.

Beau's chief competition came to grief on a jump Beau had taken easily, a high fence directly in front of shrubbery. He dislodged a rail and for several seconds refused to go on.

"That's one of the trickiest kinds of jump," Rowena commented, joining us to watch the competition till her next turn.

"Worse than the water jump?"

"Nothing's worse than the water jump," Rowena said fervently.

"How do you think it's going?" I asked.

"Good."

I noticed that other spectators and riders, out of deference to Rowena's concentration, smiled and nodded but did not try to start a conversation. Soon Rowena's turn came again, and she left wordlessly. This time Beauvais had no trouble at all.

In midafternoon there was a break—for tea, no less, served from silver urns. Spectators helped themselves to tea and pastries and circulated, chatting. I started toward the participants' circle. Tim caught my arm.

"Let her alone. She needs to be alone now."

"How do you know so much about horse meets?"

"I've picked it up," Tim said vaguely. The sound of a trumpet came over the loudspeaker, and he steered me back toward the stands.

By now it was clear that the real contest was between Rowena and a man from Virginia riding a big chestnut. The Virginian's total time was fifteen seconds less than Rowena's, and this heat ended in a tie. Tim squinted.

"Is it just me, or is Beauvais favoring his left foreleg?"

"Oh, Tim, no."

"Don't go jumping to conclusions," Tim warned. "It doesn't mean the Unicorn Curse has struck."

"Don't joke about it!"

"I'm not," Tim said gently. But his face looked sober.

There was a trumpet fanfare, then the announcer's voice. "Final heat. The contestants are ..." He reeled off names of riders and their mounts, each with their cumulative time. "For this heat, all earlier times no longer count. Each finalist starts at time zero."

Rowena, again, was the third rider. I stared tensely as she and Beau took their inspection canter. Tim was right; Beau was acting as though his leg, if not lame, were weak. Was that the same leg that had caused his downfall in the Derby? I searched my memory frantically.

As before, Rowena and Beau became immobile before beginning. Horse, rider, course, concentration were all one. Then Rowena gave some imperceptible signal, and they were off.

Beau didn't have trouble with that jump. He didn't lose any points. And when his closest competitor, the chestnut carrying the Virginian, rode last, their final time was seven seconds longer than Rowena and Beau's.

Rowena had won, and nothing had gone wrong.

I didn't know how worried I had been until I saw Rowena canter to the table that had been set up for the award ceremonies. It was adorned with a silver loving cup and—just like the Derby!—a kind of shawl of flowers. All white, very tactful; they didn't represent anyone's racing colors. Greg had diplomatically asked the president of the sponsoring company, who was his houseguest, to make the presentation, but he stood close by.

Rowena's face was beautifully composed, but her eyes, as she accepted the cup, held a mischievous twinkle. Greg looked admiring. And Beau . . . there was only one word for him as the shawl was draped around his shoulders, and that word was *conceited.* He thrust his nose in the air as if the tribute were his due, and the crowd loved it. I let out my breath and realized for the first time that my lungs were hurting.

It was over. Beau had won. Rowena and Unicorn Farm had won, because they had proved how ridiculous superstition was.

Rowena finished thanking the presenter, bowed slightly to the stands, and gave Beau a signal. They moved toward the exit, and at that moment I saw one of the Haseley Hall security police pushing through to meet her.

Even as he did, I was on my feet, out of the stand, jumping down to push through the crowd with Tim behind me.

I reached Rowena just as the security police began clearing a path for her and Beau.

"Rowena! What is it?"

"Uncle Ned's back," Rowena said tightly. "He just phoned. One of the new stallions has suddenly come down with a raging infection of some kind, and it looks bad. Uncle Ned doubts he'll live."

"I have to get there quickly," Rowena said. Her face was white. Already, spectators were pouring out of the stands and toward the parking lot, clogging the drive. A small crowd surged toward Rowena, bent on congratulations. Greg was among them.

His triumphant expression vanished as he saw her face. "What is it?" he asked anxiously.

"I can't explain now. I have to get home." For the first time in the years I'd known her, Rowena looked panicky.

"I'll drive you," Greg said immediately.

"No! You have to stay here. You have guests." Rowena's eyes darted around. Already, twilight was thickening beyond the range of the floodlights Greg had installed, and the traffic showed no sign of thinning quickly. "We couldn't get through by road, anyway. I'll ride across the fields. That will be quickest."

"Rowena, you can't! It's too dangerous," Greg protested. At the same moment, Tim cut in sharply.

"You can't do it alone. Not in the dark." He swung on Greg. "We need two more horses, for Sarah and me." He spoke with authority, and Greg responded to it.

"Yes. Of course." He gave a peremptory order to a Haseley Hall stablehand, and two riding horses were produced. They wore bridles, but no saddles.

"Don't bother, it would take too long." Tim swung himself up.

It was years since I'd ridden bareback, but I was not about to say so. The stablehand helped me mount as Greg and two of his security guards began to clear a path through the traffic.

In another moment we were beyond the rim of light and into night. Rowena, who knew the route, took the lead. Fortunately, the moon was out. It silvered the white Haseley Hall fences and the dark ones of Unicorn Farm. Beauvais galloped surely, and it came to me that he, too, knew this route very well, that Rowena must have been riding him between the two farms for some time. It came to me, too, that Rowena was very much afraid—not of this ride, but of what she would find at its end.

Rowena had spent almost a million dollars on the two new stallions, she had told me. A chill that was unrelated to the chilly weather touched my bones.

We galloped into another circle of light around the Unicorn Farm stables. In the stallion barn, Cyrus and one of the other grooms were crowded into a stall with Tom Beech and Rowena's uncle. The doctor's evil-smelling old pipe sent up a cloud of smoke that hung, somehow ominous, in the lamplit air. They all looked up as Rowena entered.

"It looks like that same mystery bacteria that got those horses last year," Beech said flatly.

Rowena was already kneeling in the straw in her immaculate jodhpurs, cradling the young animal's head in her arms. He was breathing heavily, and he looked hot.

"Where's Dr. Voelkner?" she demanded. "Haven't you even *called* him?"

"We've been phoning ever since your uncle got back and noticed something wrong. Voelkner's had a call over to Louisville. His wife's not sure where, and he won't be back till morning." The stallion manager was clearly worried. "I've been trying to raise another vet, with no luck. The point is, Rowena, if this *is* a recurrence of the earlier disease, how many people do you want to have know?"

"You think you have one chance in hell of keeping it a secret in a place like this?" Dr. Drake demanded acidly. "If you'd had half the horse sense you're getting paid for, you'd have seen the animal wasn't well hours ago, and you could have caught Voelkner before he flew the coop. It was a doggone lucky thing I happened to roll back in here when I did." He leaned against the wall, puffing malevolently. "Better get that critter into isolation before you have an epidemic on your hands."

"*Stop it,*" Rowena shouted. Her fingers were gently exploring the young horse's body. She reached his right foreleg and looked up in alarm. "This swelling at the joints. Isn't this the same . . . ?"

"Yep, and Tapestry may be showing signs of it too," Tom Beech affirmed. "Massive buildup of whatever Voelkner called it last time. It's got to be drained fast, before the poison gets into the bloodstream." He shot a glance of acute dislike toward

Dr. Drake. "You'd think that wouldn't be beyond the professional skills of our medical expert, here, but he refuses."

I was looking at Rowena's uncle, and I saw his face go gray. "I no longer practice medicine, and I am not, in any event, a horse doctor, as you damn well know, you quack!"

"If you don't have the guts to be part of the solution, then don't add to the problem," Rowena said evenly. "Get out of here, Uncle Ned. I mean it."

To my surprise he did as he was told, without bravado.

"Shouldn't we call Greg?" I asked awkwardly. "*He* could probably find a vet—"

"*No!*" Rowena checked herself. "Not unless we have to. Under the circumstances, I'd rather not."

Because of who Greg was, what she was to him, and his high-handedness? Or because of the danger of infection, and of rumors? Or—the question intruded itself into my uneasy mind—because of something more?

Tim cleared his throat. "There's a professor at the university—I've gotten kind of friendly with him. He doesn't have a veterinary practice anymore, but his specialty is endocrinological diseases. I have his home phone number. Shall I call him?"

"Please," Rowena said with relief. "Then you can go. Take Sarah back to the house and get yourselves something to eat."

"What about you?" I looked at her closely. "I'll bet you didn't even have lunch. Tim can bring us something. I'd rather stay with you here."

Rowena shook her head. "I don't want anything. I'll probably stay out here all night. Please, Sarah, I have enough to worry about. Just go."

We went. Tim telephoned his professor, Dr. Lang, from the house, where it was quieter. When Dr. Lang said he'd come right over, Tim buzzed the barn and reported the news. Then we went to the kitchen and rummaged for our supper. Or, rather, Tim did; he built a fire, parked me by it, and concocted one of his masterpieces. We ate by candlelight, and it was quite romantic—except that we were both worrying about what was happening out back.

Not ten minutes after Tim's phone call we saw the headlights of a car coming up the drive, and knew the veterinary professor had arrived. Both of us wanted to go out back, but Rowena's orders had been firm. Both of us wanted, as the evening went on, to phone for bulletins, but we didn't dare.

"Why wouldn't Dr. Drake lance the infection?" I asked suddenly.

"You'd better ask him that. Or your cousin." Tim's eyes were inscrutable.

"Do *you* know?"

"No. But it did seem weird. Almost as if he'd rather the poor horse died."

The words hung in the air, gathering significance by our sudden silence.

By eleven P.M. there was still no news. Tim looked at me. "Why don't you go to bed. If I hear anything in the bunkhouse, I'll call you."

He left after putting the dishes into the dishwasher, and I climbed the stairs into dimness. The house, with only me in it, seemed to have taken on a life of its own, a brooding waiting. I went to bed, and in a half-sleep found myself reliving those last days of Mother's final coma.

It must have been hours later when I awakened.

The house was very cold. The floor creaked in the room below me. I slipped into my robe and slippers and hurried out.

"Rowena?" I called. There was no answer. A fan of light came from the back parlor as I went downstairs, but the room was empty. She must be in the dining room, I thought; a faint clinking came from beyond its door, which was ajar.

I pushed the door open. Dr. Drake was standing at the sideboard, pouring something from a cut-glass decanter.

"Is that a good idea?" I asked levelly. It was none of my business, but surprisingly, his usually caustic tongue was silent. He just turned to look at me morosely, then he saluted me with the glass and drained it slowly. He was gazing above the sideboard, at an old painting of one of Unicorn Farm's legendary champions.

"Did my niece send you to keep an eye on me?" he asked at last.

"I doubt if she knows you're home. I didn't."

"Then spare me your reproaches." He threw himself heavily into one of the Empire dining chairs. "No doubt you are full of questions regarding that contretemps in the sick bay earlier. Sit down."

"No, I—"

"Sit down. Since you are important to Rowena, I should prefer you not to think any worse of me than you do already."

It went through my mind that if I stayed, maybe I could keep him from further drinking. I sat down guardedly. To my relief he made no move for a refill; he contemplated his filthy fingernails and began speaking in a sonorous monotone.

"I received my medical degree from Duke Uni-

versity with high honors. Oh, yes. Despite my father's dire predictions of ignominious failure as a
result of student high jinks and high living. My
father was puritanical, and to my regret Rowena
has inherited the tendency. Actually, I was rather
brilliant as a young physician, but it bored me. Of
course, I never expected a necessity ..."

His voice droned into incoherence for a few
minutes, then cleared again. He turned to me directly, and to my surprise his eyes had cleared as
well. They looked straight at me, and were full
of—what? Self-reproach? Regret? Then he said distinctly, "A few years ago, when I was practicing
both medicine and carousing on a regular basis, I
awoke one afternoon from a historic bender to
discover I had given a fellow reveler a shot destined
to remove the effects of both inebriation and hang-
over. Only I had made an error in the pharmaceuti-
cals involved. The discovery rendered me soberer
than I had been for years. I signed myself into a
hospital for what is euphemistically called a rest
cure, and I have not touched the practice of medicine since. Nor will I."

He gestured toward his empty glass. "Nor have I
touched the hair of the dog that bit me. Except one
night at a party, when some humorist thought it
amusing to doctor my ginger ales with vodka."

He stopped abruptly, his eyes staring into space.
Then he shook himself. "When I came out of the
blackout, it was three days later. I ran like a Derby
winner straight for another rest cure, and it worked.
Since then nary a drop of hooch has passed my lips.
Until tonight. Under the circumstances, with Unicorn Farm on the brink of slipping out of the family
due to my niece's stubbornness, I feel this one

drink was fully justified, medicinally. I do not propose to have another. I am not, contrary to popular opinion, an alcoholic."

He hauled himself to his feet and lumbered upstairs. After a minute I took the glass to the kitchen, washed it, and put it away. When I thought I'd given Dr. Drake enough time to fall asleep, I went back to bed.

I did not wake till sunlight was flooding brightly through my windows. I sat up abruptly, staring at the clock. Ten A.M.— I had slept clear through breakfast. I dressed quickly in stable clothes, and ran downstairs. As I did so, Rowena's voice called to me from the study.

"Is that you, Sarah? Come in, dear."

She was sitting at her desk, dressed in a tailored suit. At the sight of it my heart gave a jerk. "Rowena?"

"It was the mystery bacteria. We had to put the poor horse down. Dr. Lang's arranged for a colleague to do an autopsy at the university. Perhaps this time we'll be able to come closer to the causative factor."

"Oh, Rowena."

She looked exhausted; she looked drained bloodless. The silver cup from the horse show sat on the desk, forgotten in a ray of sunlight.

I sat down slowly, my head whirling. "Rowena . . . you went into debt to buy the horses, didn't you? What will you do?" I knew she had been depending on future stud fees and race winnings from the two-year-olds. Then something else struck me. "Your uncle said something about an epidemic—"

"We don't think we'll have to worry. The stablehands that work that barn have disinfected it thoroughly already. We do it as a routine between matings during breeding season. Fortunately there was no other horse in that barn yesterday; one thing we do know about this illness is that it has a very short gestation period. We've isolated Tapestry, just in case. And I've ordered everyone who was in contact with the animal to burn the garments that they wore there." Rowena's beautiful riding habit, I thought sadly. "I'll want what you had on last night, too, from the skin out. I assume you showered as soon as you got back here."

"Yes. With a lot of scrubbing. Tim went to the bunkhouse to shower, too, before coming up here."

"Good. Then we needn't worry about your being carriers. One blessing to count." Rowena smiled faintly.

"Rowena, what about the money you've lost?" I leaned forward. "You said I had money coming to me from Mother. Can't I—"

"Don't even think it," Rowena said firmly. Her eyes softened. "I'm touched you thought of it, love, but there's no need. I'm going into town first thing tomorrow morning to see my lawyer and my insurance agent. We have insurance coverage that I'm paying through the nose for since the—accidents. Besides, it's likely the loss will be covered by the insurance of the breeder I bought the horse from. He was warranted in good health at time of purchase."

"What about Bright Dancer?" I asked reluctantly.

"You mean could he have caught it from her if she had the mystery bacteria?" Rowena shook her head. "The bacteria has an extremely short life span outside of the animal's bloodstream, and Dancer was put down before the Saratoga shipment arrived. Besides, there's been no local outbreak of the bacteria since our earlier episode. It must have been brought in then from outside, and all the horses brought here for boarding or breeding since then have been *very* carefully inspected ..."

Rowena's voice faltered for only a moment. "So the most logical explanation is that the bacteria was brought here somehow by the two-year-old. In that case—"

She left the rest unfinished. In that case, not only would the insurance company reimburse Rowena for her lost investment, but the malady would clearly have come from outside Unicorn Farm. Not from, as Cyrus was probably already saying, a curse on Unicorn Farm.

The ray of sunlight had moved off the silver cup. It rested now on the brass unicorn. It was intended as a paperweight, and the rearing figure, at once strong yet delicate, really was quite lovely.

At that moment, owing to some trick of light, its face was grotesquely grinning.

*N*othing was the same after that. Things were happening on two levels. On the public level, Unicorn Farm was in the news in a positive way. Because of Gregory Stahl's high profile, media people had been at the horse show making notes and snapping pictures for society as well as horseracing publications. Rowena Drake, former jockey and heiress of Unicorn Farm (and its legendary curse), winning the horse show on her equally celebrated and star-crossed stallion, Beauvais, was good news. Rowena's public relations agency, of course, played it up in press releases and advertising.

On the private level, a whole different scenario was unrolling, a scenario of insurance inspectors and veterinarians, laboratory technicians and researchers. Dr. Lang, having been called in, could hardly forget what he had observed. Fortunately, he agreed that secrecy was necessary until the precise nature of the bacteria involved had been determined.

And then there was Greg. Greg arrived on the scene right after my talk with Rowena, looking stern.

"I got rid of my guests as quickly as I could without arousing unnecessary questions. Rowena, what is wrong? Do not try to shut me out this time, because I will not let you."

And Rowena told him. I knew, because I was there, at her request. My presence both signaled my position at Unicorn Farm and prevented her scene with Greg from veering off in personal directions. He nodded when he heard about Tim's professor.

"I have heard of the man. One of the best equine physicians since the late Dr. Jenny and his pioneer work in healing racehorses' broken bones, and highly respected for his endocrinology research." His eyes narrowed. "Interesting that your part-time stablehand should be acquainted with him. I should have thought the doctor far removed from association with undergraduates."

It was a thought that had occurred to me.

Rowena brushed all that aside. "The main point is, he may be able to identify the bacteria, if it *is* the one that caused the deaths here before. I wish this man had been at the university then! He's arranged for the autopsy on this stallion, and says one must be done on the remains of Bright Dancer, too. And I've given him all the records from the earlier episodes." She walked to the study window and stood staring out at the great bare trees. "My main worry is whether Tapestry has the virus too. Greg, I'm so afraid—"

Greg went over and put his arms around her, and I decided I'd played chaperone long enough.

I went outside and around to the stables, where the morning routine had been completed. The sun was shining, and life was going on. K.T. hailed me from the exercise ring, where she was supervising one of the new fillies.

"Tapestry's much better today, I'm happy to say. One worry less. I still have no idea what caused the lameness, but it's not infection."

There was no point in trying to keep secrets from K.T. "You know what happened?"

K.T. nodded. "I wouldn't let my imagination run wild if I were you," she advised. "Bacterial infections don't just pop up out of nowhere! This one has to have been transmitted in some recognized fashion, by blood or injection, or by mating, or possibly from something in the feed. It wasn't just blowing in the wind into the animals' bloodstreams!"

In other words, it wasn't from some old curse, or lingering in the stable walls. "Good thing Bright Dancer was buried on the grounds," she added. "The other horses that died weren't Unicorn Farm animals."

I knew it was customary to bury head, heart, and hooves of notable horses on the grounds of their home stables. Rowena had already ordered a grave marker for Bright Dancer. How fortunate that it had not already been installed. I avoided the small graveyard beyond the orchard, where the clink of shovels could be heard.

Rowena saw her lawyer. Her insurance company, and the insurance companies of the people who had bred her Saratoga purchases, all sent inspectors and veterinarians. I gathered that top-level research and conferences were going on in laboratories somewhere. In the meantime, Tapestry was kept isolated until it was clear he was in excellent health. The veterinarians intimated that his condition could have been caused by some kind of drug. Dr. Voelkner and Tom Beech both bristled at that.

Astonishingly, no rumor about the situation had leaked out at all. The stablehands seemed bound by a code of silence that even held, Tim told me, when they were out drinking. Dr. Drake was mute and apprehensive. Greg, when quizzed about Rowena and her sudden departure from the horse show, managed to be charming but evasive.

I went to classes. I worked around the farm and went riding on Jeeter. I tried to cheer Rowena, who acted as though she didn't need it. And Tim and I went out a few times, but we got into an argument that seemed impossible to resolve.

It happened because I was alarmed about the way Rowena, while showing her usual warmth and compassion, was so controlled. Except for that moment with Greg in the study, she never broke. She said no more to me about the curse or about the circumstances of the fire, and there was no way I could bring those subjects up. Not now. Under Rowena's outer layer of practical worries was an imperturbable serenity, and under that was—what?

It troubled me; it sometimes frightened me. I confided in Tim while we were having dinner together (alone) in the bunkhouse.

Tim looked at me inscrutably. "Runs in the family, doesn't it?"

"What does?"

"Hanging on to your self-control. No matter what." He allowed a beat of silence to hang between us. "Rowena still hasn't come to terms with the implications of what's going on here, starting with the fire. *You* haven't come to terms with your mother's death."

"You've got a nerve," I said when I could speak.

"Have I?" Tim countered. "I saw you arrive here three days after your mother's funeral. I've been with you most of every day since, and you've never talked about it, you've never cracked."

"That's because I had several months to come to terms with it before it happened," I answered coldly.

Tim looked at me for several seconds. "Okay. If you say so," he said at last. He leaned over and kissed me.

It wasn't till a day or so later that it dawned on me what Tim had said about things going on here *starting with the fire*.

The results of the autopsies and other lab work came in. The evidence from Bright Dancer's remains was inconclusive. The new stallion had suffered from a bacteria as yet unidentified, but whether it was the same one that caused the deaths that prior year or the sickness that doomed Dancer was not yet clear. In any event, since Dancer died before the new stock's arrival, and since the bacteria was not active in any Unicorn Farm horses when they *did* arrive, there was no discernible way the stallion could have been infected here at Unicorn Farm. The scientists recommended that the company insuring the breeder of the dead stallion should reimburse Rowena the purchase price.

Tapestry didn't come down with the bacteria. The other Saratoga horses didn't come down with the bacteria. Neither did any other horses at Unicorn Farm.

Things settled down; even Dr. Drake was subdued. We began looking forward to Thanksgiving.

There remained the problem of replacing Gilfillan, the trainer. Rowena talked to him, and he was regretful but adamant. "At this point in my life and work I just don't need that kind of aggravation, Miss Drake. I'm sorry." He added pointed advice that Rowena convince her uncle to move back to his New York apartment permanently.

"I wish I could!" Rowena said when she told me about the conversation.

"Why can't you?" I asked bluntly.

"The problem is whether he'd start drinking. I wouldn't want it on my conscience I drove him back to that."

I still didn't say anything about that night in the dining room. Dr. Drake's words about that being a one-time aberrance had had the ring of truth. What was more to the point, so had his behavior since.

Rowena looked for a trainer, but those available didn't meet her standards. I suspected she was stalling, hoping to save money by doing the job herself. She was working too hard, and she was growing thin.

In mid-November Greg paid one of his characteristically unexpected visits, arriving this time not on Maximilian but in an equally black Mercedes. "This situation is ridiculous. I have found you a trainer, at least an interim trainer," he said calmly, overriding her protest. "His name's Luke Hoyle. He's half-Irish, like Gilfillan, and he's been working in Ireland for the past few years. He was recommended to me by friends there. He's flying over tomorrow and will come straight here."

"I can't pay to fly a European trainer over here! Are you mad?" Rowena exclaimed.

"His ticket is already bought. Moreover, I have taken the liberty of advancing him his first six months salary. So you cannot discharge him until that time is up. My company will expect to be reimbursed by Unicorn Farm at that time; by then the breeding and foaling seasons will be over, so you should have no trouble." Greg looked at his watch. "By now the man is already aboard his plane, and I am sure you do not intend to pay for his round trip for nothing. So there is really nothing much you can do except say thank you."

Rowena, faced with a choice of emotions for responding, chose to laugh. "Oh, all right! It's nearly Thanksgiving, so I suppose I should be gracious. But I want a formal loan agreement between Unicorn Farm and your company."

"I have it right here," Greg said blandly.

Luke Hoyle duly arrived, and Tim, who'd been sent to meet him at the airport, provided me with the best description of him: "He's a personality—as if we didn't have enough of them here already, between the people and the horses."

He was putting it diplomatically. The word for Luke Hoyle, like the word for Dr. Drake, was *character.* I reserved the right to decide later whether it was good or bad. Not that Hoyle was like Rowena's Uncle Ned; far from it. He was wiry and rugged; he reminded me more of Mel Gibson than of the tough little Irishmen I'd met around the horse world. Except he couldn't quite be called handsome. A tan cigarette perpetually dangled from his lips, but he obeyed Rowena's injunction not to smoke in the barns. He was abrasive enough to get the stable staff's backs up, knowledgeable enough to earn their respect.

"He knows horses," K.T. told me emphatically. "He knows when to be gentle with them and when to be tough."

I suspected, after I saw the expert way he sized us all up, that he knew women too. He treated Rowena as the boss, me as the boss's relative, and K.T. as a fellow expert. I also suspected, from a lot of things I could not pin down, that he was coming on to K.T. on other levels too.

Rowena's attitude on Hoyle was mixed. "I have to admit I'm glad to have him," she confided. "He's doing a good job with Tapestry." I knew Rowena was planning to race him this coming spring. "But I'll be darned if I intend to put up with being patronized! It's bad enough taking that from Cyrus." This was after Luke and Rowena had had a difference of opinion over Beauvais's feeding and routine.

There was one thing we both agreed was good about Luke Hoyle: He was close-mouthed. Just as we heard little about the man himself, no one heard anything from him about the curse on Unicorn Farm, though he must have found out about it around the stable.

November sped toward December as the lawyers and insurance companies dragged their feet. Thanksgiving came. K.T. went home to her family in Middleburg, Virginia. Tim went home to New York State, and Unicorn Farm seemed bleak to me without him. Greg Stahl came to Unicorn Farm for Thanksgiving dinner.

It suddenly hit me, that morning, that this was my first holiday without my mother, and that I would never have another one again. No Thanksgivings, no Fourth of Julys, no Christmases. No birthdays; no graduation—I wasn't even going to have a high school graduation.

I remembered what Tim had said that time we nearly fought, and thought that he didn't know us

Burtons very well. It had hit me, and I was facing it, and what I felt was not a sorrow but a numbness.

The numbness passed with the morning. The sun was bright, and an illusion of summer hung over the Kentucky fields. Rowena and I went riding. In the late afternoon Greg came. We dined by candlelight in the dining room with its dark green flocked Victorian wallpaper, its fruitwood and ebony Empire furniture, its brass and crystal. Rowena wore black velvet. I wore a soft cinnamon-colored silk dress that I'd bought with my own money, and wished that Tim were there.

Then it was December, and things began to crumble. Not with the horses—thank God, not with the horses. But Luke Hoyle was becoming overbearing. One of the grooms quit. Cyrus made noises, that neither Rowena nor I believed, about retiring. A week later, when I was writing a term paper on the computer in the business office, Tim came in, looking out of breath. "Where's Miss D?"

He put it that way because Helen Gallagher, Rowena's red-haired secretary, was present. She swiveled around at once at the note in his voice. "Over at Haseley, I think. What's happened?"

"Hoyle threatened to have Cyrus sacked, and Dr. Drake got into the middle of it. Tom Beech is holding them all apart. Rowena'd better come."

He ran out again. Helen's fingers were already busy at the telephone. I wanted to run after Tim but decided it would only make things worse. Shortly afterward, Rowena's car zoomed in. It passed the office and went directly to the training rink.

When she came into the office sometime later, her lips were tight, and Helen and I discreetly minded our own business. I heard an account of the epi-

sode later, anyway, from Tim. Rowena had made
very clear to all present that *she* was the sole owner
of Unicorn Farm, and she alone made personnel
decisions. She also reminded Luke that he had a
six-month contract he couldn't break without financial penalty, a little item I hadn't heard about before. I mentally thanked Greg for his foresight.

I felt less like thanking Greg that evening. Tim
and I were in the kitchen making fudge when Greg
arrived to see Rowena. They were in the front parlor, already decked with its Victorian Christmas
garlands and Della Robbia wreaths. The manor house
was old, with correspondingly thick walls, but voices
carried, thanks to an antiquated system of heating
ducts. What Greg was saying made me color to the
roots of my hair.

"I am warning you, Rowena, if you continue like
this, you are creating an incendiary situation."

"Are you threatening me, Gregory?" Rowena inquired with deceptive calm.

"Not threatening. Warning you, as a friend should.
I use that name for myself since you will not allow
me one more intimate. You should retire Cyrus,
exactly as Hoyle suggests. You cannot help knowing he is the root cause of half the suspicions circulating about Unicorn Farm!"

"And the other half?" Rowena asked in that
same calm voice.

"Who else? Your uncle! It humiliates him to be
living here on his niece's charity. You are completely right, your father and your grandfather were
right, Ned Drake is totally unfit to run anything. But
he could at least own some of it! Do you know
what you Drakes have done here, Rowena? You
have set up a feudal dynasty . . . strong-willed peo-

ple, locked by blood and more, only one of which can be the king or queen! At least in Europe we have primogeniture! The eldest son knows he will inherit all; the rest of us plan from childhood to make our own ways elsewhere. Give Ned a piece of the place, or send him off!"

"You know I can't," Rowena said stubbornly.

Greg went on as if she hadn't spoken. "And Sarah! You are doing the same thing with her. Taking someone in as a dependent because you love them, you want to take care of them. Forgetting that dependency creates two things—strong energies with no sane channel for them, or else weakness. Make them a part of things, or let them live their own lives!"

His voice changed, softened. "Or sell the whole damn place to me, and get rid of the problem once and for all."

"You know I won't do that," Rowena repeated. But her voice, too, had softened.

Tim and I heard Greg laugh. "At least close this place down for Christmas and come to Switzerland with me! You can bring Sarah. We can go skiing in the Alps and let our employees worry about the horses. Rowena, do say yes. You can come with me on the plane tomorrow."

Their voices became indistinguishable. I felt hot all over. Tim, after a swift glance at me, looked away and said briskly, "Let's go into town and catch a late movie. Neither one of us has morning classes."

I did not tell Rowena what we'd heard, and Rowena said nothing about Greg's visit, either. She did put on a good suit and drive into town the next afternoon without explanation. Whether she saw Greg then or not, I didn't know. Her face was stoic.

Tim learned later from the stable grapevine that Greg Stahl had flown to Europe that night for the Christmas holidays.

By now signs of Christmas were everywhere. Store windows blossomed; the old restored section of Lexington flaunted its bright banners. Town houses showed wreaths and candles in their windows. There was a dinner-dance at the country club; Rowena took Tim and me. Rowena and I picked out a Christmas tree. We trimmed it before Tim left for New York State; it stood in the front hall, glowing against the gold-foil Chinese wallpaper, picking up the jewel tones in the Oriental rug. There were garlands of greens around the pillars dividing the hall from the two parlors, and garlands down the banisters.

I remembered the decorations packed away somewhere back in Connecticut. I didn't say so.

Tim left, promising to write. I promised too. I saw Tim off at the airport, and we kissed good-bye, but the parting nonetheless was strained. Too much was unresolved between us. Or was it that too much was unresolved inside ourselves?

Rowena and I were alone in the manor house for a few days, for Dr. Drake had taken himself off on one of his periodic jaunts to Lord-knew-where. He came home in time for Christmas, and Christmas was happier than I expected. We all went to midnight service. We had breakfast together in the kitchen around the fire, a lavish country breakfast. We opened presents, and had midday dinner, and after that the Unicorn Farm workers and their families dropped in for fruitcake, eggnog, and mulled wine.

When they were gone, Rowena went to stand

before the fireplace and looked at me and at her uncle.

"I have something to say, and I want to say it now. Things that have happened lately, things people have said to me, have made me think."

For a heart-stopping moment, I thought she was going to say she was selling Unicorn Farm.

What she did say was that she had taken Greg's earlier advice, and incorporated Unicorn Farm as a business, and that she was giving nonvoting shares of stock to Uncle Ned and me.

Dr. Drake was as stunned as I was. He changed color twice and ended looking somehow grayer than before.

"You shouldn't have," I managed when I found my voice. "Unicorn Farm is *yours*. I never expected . . . you certainly didn't have to give me any of it!"

Involuntarily my eyes flickered toward Ned Drake. If Rowena understood why, she gave no sign. "I know I didn't have to," she said, smiling. "That's not why I did it. Greg's advice was sound—it was time to incorporate."

The slight stress she put on that last word effectively ruled out his other advice about selling, syndicating, or both. Then she laughed. "You needn't be too grateful! Those shares may not be worth much if our streak of bad luck continues. In any event, there's a clause in the legal papers giving me the first option on buying them back if either of you wants to sell."

"If you'd given me voting stock," Dr. Drake said heavily, "I'd have voted to go into syndication."

"I'm well aware of that," Rowena said.

The whole thing left me with mixed feelings. I knew Rowena had given the shares to me out of love. And to Uncle Ned out of what? Guilt, two generations removed? Protectiveness, hoping to lift his depression? Or for reassurance?

I wondered if I should have told Rowena about her uncle and the liquor decanter. But he hadn't drunk a thing on Christmas Day. I also wished that Dr. Drake and Greg Stahl had kept their mouths shut about my relationship to Rowena and Unicorn Farm. I'd have preferred the gift of part ownership, if it came at all, to be her own idea.

The Christmas celebration broke up early. Rowena went for a drive with friends to look at other people's Christmas decorations. Dr. Drake stomped up to the third floor to his study, a dim slant-walled space that reminded me, the one time I'd seen it, of an attic out of Dickens. I went to my room and turned on the TV, but I had too much to think about to pay it much attention.

The Christmas holidays seemed strange this year, and not just because my mother wasn't there. I wasn't in high school, I was taking only nine hours of college classes a week, so I didn't feel now as if I were on vacation. And of course, holidays or no holidays, the daily farm routines prevailed. On Christmas morning, as usual, I'd helped exercise the horses, and done my share of mucking out and currying. I continued to do so, the only difference from usual being that Tim wasn't there. I missed him more than I'd dreamed I could.

In the days that followed, I noticed that Mr. Beech was just managing to keep peace in the stables. I noticed something else too. Luke seemed to be picking arguments with K.T. that were part come-on, part insult, part challenge. "I don't know how you put up with it," I exclaimed to K.T. when I'd been a witness to one of these exchanges on the twenty-eighth. K.T. grinned.

"About the same way you put up with Tim Payne, I imagine. You two sound a lot like that yourselves at times, or haven't you noticed?"

I didn't think it the time to point out that Tim didn't patronize me, and had a lot better manners. We were in the business office, and both Rowena and Helen Gallagher were within earshot. At that moment the telephone rang; Helen answered, then put it on hold and looked at me with mischief.

"Speak of the devil. It's Tim. You can take it in Rowena's office if you want," she added unnecessarily, for I was already on my way in there.

I shut the door and picked up the receiver. "Tim, hi!"

"Hi, Sarah." Tim sounded a bit odd, but I put that down to the long distance line. "Look, I'm coming back to Kentucky earlier than I expected. Do you already have a date for New Year's Eve, or do you suppose we could do something?"

"I suppose we could," I replied, trying to sound as laid back as he. I couldn't have been altogether successful, for he laughed and sounded a lot more cheerful.

"*All right!* See you sometime the afternoon of the thirtieth. I'm not sure what I'll be able to do about planes."

"You could have dinner here on New Year's and watch TV or the VCR if you want to," Rowena said when she heard all this. "Greg just called; he'll be back on the thirty-first, and we're going to a party. You'd have the house to yourselves."

"What about your uncle?"

"Didn't I tell you? He got a phone call from some man this morning and then announced he was leaving immediately for a week or so. He didn't say where." Rowena frowned. "He isn't acting like himself, not even the self he's been lately. I'd better make a New Year's resolution to get to the bottom of that right after the holidays."

"What about a resolution to get to the bottom of your feelings for Greg Stahl?" I asked daringly.

"Don't start," Rowena retorted. Perhaps deliberately, she didn't raise the matter of my feelings for Tim Payne.

They were, to say the very least, mixed. I liked him—a lot. And yet ... *something* ... held me back from really letting down my barriers with him.

I wondered if that held true for Rowena with Greg, as well.

Rowena insisted, despite the precarious state of Unicorn Farm's finances, on buying New Year's Eve clothes for both of us. We went to a specialty shop downtown and found lovely things. Rowena's was black velvet, long, boat-necked, and deceptively simple except for its side slit and jeweled embroidery. The gold and copper beads brought out the copper highlights in her hair. For me Rowena found a dark green cut velvet that made me think of our dining room wallpaper and made me look like a Renaissance contessa.

"It's too formal for a night at home," I objected.

"Why can't that be formal? The dress goes with the manor house. Eat in the dining room; it looks very romantic by candlelight," Rowena recommended, her eyes twinkling. "Tim's always eating, not to mention cooking, in our kitchen so *that* should be pretty exciting for him."

On December thirtieth a few strange things happened. Rowena was away most of the day, but that wasn't particularly unusual. I found out K.T. was going out with Luke on New Year's Eve, and that wasn't surprising, either. What *was* surprising was the uncomfortable exchange I had with K.T. on the subject.

I had told K.T. all about my telephone call from Tim, and on the early afternoon of the thirtieth I was walking Tapestry round and round the horses' swimming pool while talking to her about the problem I was having with Tim. K.T. was acting like a big sister, taking it all in with wise comments while revealing nothing. Luke walked through in the middle of this, ignoring me completely, ignoring even K.T. till he was at the other door. Then he threw back across his shoulder, "Be ready at seven tomorrow night. We're going to drive over to a bash in Louisville."

When he was gone I turned to K.T. in exasperation. "Nice of him to tell you instead of ask you!" Then I took in the expression on her face. It was a mixture of defensiveness, pride—and something else. I realized with a sinking heart that K.T. had really fallen for Luke Hoyle.

"You've had this date with him all along, haven't you?" I asked. I didn't add, as I could have, *But you never told me.*

K.T. responded to what I'd left unspoken. "I know you don't like Luke. You know, in a way you're very sheltered, Sarah. I know Luke's rough, but that's just typical of guys from the racing world. I understand that world."

And you don't, yet. . . . That was the implication.

I went to the stallion barn afterward to give Beau and Tapestry their peppermint treats. I gave Tapestry his first; I was trying to teach him Beau's trick of flipping the mint with his tongue before eating it. The extension telephone rang while I was there. This was the main, listed Unicorn phone number, and it reached all farm buildings; we also had an unlisted number for the manor house.

It rang five times, and I realized that everyone else must have gone home and that Rowena was still out. I picked up the receiver and said, "Unicorn Farm."

A male voice asked for Dr. Drake.

"He's not here," I said. "Can I take a message?"

The voice insisted on knowing when he would be back and, when I said he was away, where he had gone. "I really don't know," I answered, nettled. "Would you like to leave—"

The caller hung up.

"Who was that?" Luke demanded from the far doorway.

He was wearing boots, but I hadn't hear him approach. I jumped. "It wasn't for you," I responded shortly.

"That's not what I asked you." Luke strode over, and as I turned to give Beau his peppermint, he grabbed my hand.

"I don't want you giving those things to the horses! There are notices giving my instructions posted on the bulletin board. Don't you ever read them?"

I jerked away, my eyes blazing. "Beau likes peppermints, and Rowena likes for him to have them. You may be head trainer, but you're not training Beau."

"No, he doesn't race anymore, except in horse shows," Luke replied with sarcasm. "We all know what happened to him in the Derby when Miss Rowena Drake was handling him! If she's not careful, she may not have him in her hands much longer."

"Is that some kind of a threat?" I asked icily.

"It's plain fact, and if you care anything about her, you'd make her realize it." Luke's face changed into a sneer. "You like butting into other people's business, don't you? Like trying to warn K. T. Healy away from me. Call this a warning, honey. Stick to your own safe little world and don't go poking into things that aren't your business. You may be the boss's cousin, but you're only a stable rat when it comes to the horse breeding business."

His contempt was so obvious that it pushed me into saying what I otherwise never would. "I may be a novice in the stable, but I'm also its part owner! And you're an employee! So you'd better—"

I broke off in mid-sentence, because Luke had suddenly, roughly, grabbed me. Not like before. His fingers bit into my arms and he swung me round to face him sharply.

"You're hurting me!" I shouted.

His face was livid. That much registered on me, and that was all, because at that moment Tim suddenly was there. He was saying, "Take your hands off her!" in a voice like brittle steel, and breaking me away from Luke with hands that were every bit as harsh as Luke's had been.

*F*or a second the two men stared each other down. It was Luke who left, turning on his heel. Tim turned to watch him, breathing hard, and I rubbed my bruised arms.

Then Tim swung on me. "Haven't you got any more sense than get into a fight with a guy like him?" he demanded. "You don't know anything about him, and you're half his size!"

I didn't want Tim to know how scared I'd been, and I didn't like his thinking me a fool. "I know a couple of things," I snapped. "He works here, and in a way he works for me. What did you think he was going to do, beat me up? Do you really think I'm such a—a wimp that I need a protector looking after me?"

"I think," Tim said carefully after a long minute, "that there's a lot more been going on here than either of us know. Maybe you've decided you can't trust me enough to share them. Or maybe you can't trust yourself enough to face them."

And with that he, too, turned on his heel and

exited. I wasn't looking forward anymore to New Year's Eve.

But I went on next day with my New Year's Eve preparations. Knowing how Tim loved pasta, I'd decided to pull out the stops with an Italian menu. Fettuccine Alfredo and veal scaloppine—fortunately I already knew how to make them. More to the point, they would need very little attention during a romantic evening. If it was still going to *be* romantic.

I didn't run into Tim at all during the day of the thirty-first, and I didn't plan to make the first move. So I kept on getting ready, setting the dining room table with heirloom family porcelain and crystal, putting fresh candles in silver candlesticks and the chandelier.

I went out briefly in the afternoon and when I returned, Rowena said Tim had called. "He wanted to know what time he should pick you up, and what you'd like to do. I told him you were planning dinner here and to come around seven. That's when Greg and I are leaving. I hope that was all right?"

"That was fine," I said in a muffled voice.

I took a shower, and put on the green cut-velvet dress, and the pearl necklace and earrings Dad had given Mother. It was the first time I'd worn them. I zipped Rowena's black velvet for her, accepted her compliments, and gave mine in return. Then I went downstairs and lit the Christmas tree and all the candles.

Greg arrived for Rowena, and they left. Tim still hadn't come. I began to wonder whether he would.

It was almost seven-thirty before the doorbell chimed. Tim stood there, his arms full of dark red roses.

"I figured if you were providing the meal, I could

provide the decorations," he said when I exclaimed. To my relief he sounded much as always, as though the scene in the barn had never happened. But there was a quietness, a kind of deep sobriety about him beneath the surface laughter that troubled me. I began to feel a faint fear over what I'd done.

That sense of a shadow over us diminished as the evening passed. Tim insisted on coming to the kitchen to help cook the scallopine. He laughed at my method, learned from my mother, of warming the cream and butter for the Alfredo sauce by setting the platter holding it on top of the boiling· pot of fettuccine. We ate in style, in the dining room, at the fruitwood and ebony Empire table.

I told him about Christmas, and how Rowena had rendered us speechless with her gifts of part ownership. For a minute I saw something flicker in his eyes. Then he smiled. "Where's the doctor to-night? Are we going to be lucky enough to be uninterrupted?"

"We don't know *where* he is. He took off right after receiving some mysterious telephone call." That led into a retelling of the phone call I'd received for him the day before. Don't say I don't trust you with things, I thought, as I was telling this. Tim didn't like the business of that call one bit, though he made a good effort to mask his reaction.

"How was your Christmas?" I asked, partly to change the subject, partly out of genuine concern. There was something—I couldn't put my finger on it—troubling Tim.

"It was okay. Not what I expected." And that was all he'd say about it.

"I suppose . . . once a big change happens, like

going away to college . . . nothing's ever quite the same."

"No. And that has to be accepted," Tim said dryly.

After dinner we took the dishes to the kitchen and watched TV in the back parlor's raspberry brocaded splendor, in honor of the holidays. And although we were closely snuggled on the sofa, there was a separation of a kind between us.

One of the networks was showing *The Best Years of Our Lives.* "That's a great old film. Let's watch it," Tim said, turning channels. The movie, about World War II veterans returning to a changed world and changed relationships, was broadcast every holiday season. Usually, I cried. Tonight nothing reached me.

"You didn't shed one tear, did you?" Tim asked me oddly when it was over.

"I've seen it before. Lots of times," I said briefly.

"And I'll bet it always got you, didn't it?" Tim said in that same voice. And then, "You still haven't faced your feelings about your mother, have you?"

All at once a cold rage was building in me. "I faced that a long time ago," I said distinctly. "Starting with the day I sat in the doctor's office and heard him tell me she wouldn't live. I've had a lot of time to get used to it. Obviously, you've never lost anybody you loved a lot, so you don't understand."

Tim didn't answer right away. "Come on," he said then in a perfectly neutral voice, "let's clean up the dinner dishes before Rowena gets home."

We put kitchen aprons on over our finery. We took the red roses into the kitchen with us, and they glowed in the kitchen firelight like dark wet blood.

Tim asked me more about Rowena's gift of Unicorn Farm stock, and everyone's responses, and I answered. I told him about my impulsive gaffe to Luke on the subject, just before he himself came charging to my rescue, and he agreed it had been unwise. "So that's what set off Hoyle," he commented. "Interesting."

"Too interesting," I muttered, rubbing my arms. I still had bruises.

Tim massaged them for me gently. "Rowena's opened a can of worms having him here."

"She didn't bring him in. Greg did." I twisted my head to look at Tim. "Why? Do you know anything about him that we don't?"

"Not yet. Not about Stahl, either." Tim turned me around and led me to the kitchen sofa. "Look, Sarah, I didn't mean to tell you about this tonight. But I'd better, because Rowena may hear something at that party."

"You're scaring me."

"I don't want to. No, maybe I do. Maybe it's necessary. Sarah, while I was on the plane yesterday I saw a syndicated sports column in a newspaper. It said there are rumors going around that the 'deadly mystery bacteria that struck star-crossed Unicorn Farm last year has struck again.' How could that rumor have gotten out? Only from people who were here when that stallion died."

And from the few outsiders not bound by Unicorn Farm loyalty, his eyes implied. Luke, the new trainer. His own professor, and his colleagues—but Tim trusted that professor implicitly. And Greg Stahl.

In the silence, the grandfather's clock in the front hall chimed the three-quarter hour. Fifteen minutes to midnight. The end of the known year.

Suddenly, the rage that had stirred in me earlier returned. "If Rowena wasn't so darn trusting!" I exclaimed. "And so stubborn! Greg was right. She shouldn't be trying to keep Unicorn Farm as it's always been, living in the past. Those days are *gone*. They've been gone, ever since the fire.... Maybe she should just sell and get out, the way Greg wants."

"Oh, so that's what he's after?" Tim asked, watching me closely.

"He's after owning Unicorn Farm, and her. He'd settle for stallion syndication. She won't face the need for doing that any more than she's facing—"

I stopped abruptly.

"What?" Tim probed. I shook my head. I could not tell him, no matter how personally he took my silence, that Rowena believed the fire had been deliberate—and the fire-related deaths accidental deaths from arson.

"She's always so calm," I said. "No matter what. As if she weren't in danger of losing everything. It's not natural."

"Not *natural?*" Tim repeated. "Like the way you can't even cry?" He took my face in his hands, forcing me to look at him. "Sarah, I know you hate hearing this. But aren't you and Rowena doing the same thing? Not going through the stages of grief? Loss of Unicorn Farm would be a kind of death, too, just like the deaths of your parents, and of hers."

"You keep harping on that!" My voice spiraled, startling me. I jumped up and moved away. "Let me tell you, Tim Payne, in the—what is it, two years? —since the fire, Rowena's had plenty of time to stop denying her parents' death and accept their being gone. She's had all that time to keep hearing about the 'curse' on Unicorn Farm! You think she hasn't faced what that means, all of it? You think I haven't faced losing Mother and all that went with it? *You* try waiting through months of somebody's terminal illness, and then you can tell me about not accepting it and the emotions that go with it!"

"You're overlooking one of them, aren't you?" Tim said quietly. "Both you and Rowena. Anger. Aren't you both—all tight-wired with anger, so tightly you can't move without hurting? About all those deaths. About what's happening to Unicorn Farm."

"You're damned right I'm angry!" I burst out. "It isn't fair! None of it is fair—" My voice thickened suddenly. "It wasn't fair that Mother suffered like that. Always being brave for my sake! It wasn't fair for Rowena's parents to get burned up—we don't even know for sure whether they were overcome by smoke, or were conscious—"

I swallowed hard. My eyes felt filled with sand. "And the horses—I overheard Uncle Gil telling my father once, long ago, how he'd heard the screams of horses in a fire. . . . And Mother and I didn't even know about the fire here when it happened; we didn't come, because Rowena was so considerate, not telegraphing us where we were on vacation. . . . Rowena's always so thoughtful, that's why it's so unfair, her being blamed for Unicorn Farm's decline. She's put everything of herself into it. She's kept going because she had to. Just as I had to. And it *isn't fair!*"

Suddenly I *was* crying, great gulping sobs, almost without my noticing. They racked me, they bent me double, until Tim came and took me in his arms and held me. Not holding me protected from the feelings, but helping me endure them.

Out in the front hall the chime clock rang the end of the old, the beginning of the new.

CHAPTER

13

For me, personally, and for my relationship with Tim, the new year marked a tremulous turning point. It was a turning point for Unicorn Farm as well. The published rumor of the return of the killer bacteria, arriving in Lexington with other travelers who had also read that newspaper column, rocked our world. From then on, things went steadily downhill.

" 'The Return of the Killer Bacteria.' It sounds like the title for a horror movie," Rowena giggled hysterically on New Year's morning. The rumor had been rampant at last night's party, and she'd come into my bedroom to serve it up to me with my morning coffee.

"Don't worry," I said with more assurance than I felt. "The results of the insurance company investigation should be in soon. They're bound to pay your claim—after all, there wasn't any of the disease on the premises when the stallion got here! And that will squelch the story."

"Don't be too sure," Rowena said soberly. "My

attorney was at the party last night. He seemed to be avoiding my eyes."

The rumor was spreading in other circles too. K.T. and Luke heard it in Louisville. Luke telephoned Rowena at home early in the afternoon to literally demand an interview with her first thing the next morning. Rowena dealt with him shortly. Soon after that, Mr. Beech arrived in person, looking grim. He and his family had heard the story at morning Mass, and he wanted to know how Rowena wanted him to answer questions.

"You know the situation. Just stall as much as you can, and try to look optimistic," Rowena said wearily. She was not following her own instructions very well.

Usually, Rowena had told me, there was general visiting back and forth on New Year's afternoon. This year, few people came. Shortly before four, Greg drove up and peremptorily kidnapped Rowena. "We'll go for a drive. Not visiting! And you and Sarah will dine at Haseley Hall. I've instructed the security guards to keep the gates locked to all comers."

Ordinarily Rowena would have been irritated by his high-handedness, but not today. They drove off. Taking a leaf out of Greg's book, I locked our doors and turned off the hanging brass lantern above the entrance. I went upstairs and changed out of my good dress into jeans, and thought about the curse on Unicorn Farm, and about last night.

Soon after that, the doorbell chimed. And kept on chiming, even though I ignored it. It stopped. A few minutes later the telephone rang. Tim's voice demanded, "Why didn't you let me in?"

"I didn't know it was you."

"Well, it was. Come around back. I'm in the barn, and I've got Jeeter saddled."

More high-handedness, but I, too, didn't mind. We went for a ride through the deepening winter darkness, and a damp mist stung our faces, and the tightness that had been coiling in my chest began unwinding. My barriers had come down so abruptly last night, we'd gone so fast to such depth of sharing feelings, that I'd been half afraid of seeing Tim again. It was good to have our next meeting be like this, riding side by side, feeling each other's nearness without much talking. When we returned to the manor house Tim kissed me lightly, and then not so lightly, but would not come in.

The Mercedes parked in the driveway indicated that Rowena and Greg were back. I took a quick shower, got dressed up again, and went with them to Haseley Hall for dinner. There were just the three of us. The dining room, which was done in some decorator's idea of international playboy, was a wonder, and so was the food. But I couldn't describe anything we ate, or talked about.

The Louisville newspaper of January second carried guarded rebuttals by Mr. Beech and Rowena's lawyer, and said that "Rowena Drake, the former jockey, and heiress to the historic farm of which until recently she was sole owner," had not been available for comment.

"So they found about the stock transfer," Rowena said, putting the paper carefully aside. "I wonder how. Some bright reporter did some digging at the state capital, I suppose!"

She didn't say, nor did I, one thing that was foremost in our minds: Thank goodness Dr. Ned Drake, disinherited and disgruntled family member, was nowhere around. We still didn't know where he was, and that was just as well. On January third that same male voice called back demanding to speak to him.

"He can't be anywhere close, or we'd have heard about it," Rowena said frankly. "Maybe we're lucky and he's gone abroad! Though I can't imagine how he could afford it."

The real import of the rumor didn't hit me right away, partly because I was still new to the horse world and partly because I was suddenly very busy. Attending college, even part-time, was a lot different from high school. There had been, to my delight, no steady diet of homework, exams, and quizzes. Now, however, the end of the semester suddenly loomed. I faced a term paper for each of my three classes, plus three two-hour-long exams. It was panic time.

Maybe I was panicking about schoolwork rather than about the fate of Unicorn Farm, but I doubted it. Since New Year's Eve, I was recognizing, and admitting to myself, the exact nature of my complicated feelings. I knew for sure now that I didn't want to go back to high school, ever; I didn't want to go away to college, either. I wanted to stay here, and work with Rowena and with horses. And now that I was a part owner of Unicorn Farm, learn more about horse farm management. Which meant I had to pass these courses with flying colors, and get accepted as a full-time student.

So I crammed, sometimes with Tim's help, sometimes alone. I approached Helen Gallagher to see if I could write the term papers on the office computer, and she agreed gladly. "If you know how to run this darn thing, maybe you could take over maintaining the breeding records Rowena wants kept on it."

"I'd love to," I said. "What kind of records?"

"Oh, bloodlines, and stud fees, and breeding appointments, that sort of thing. Rowena's eager to get all the past records entered, back to when Beauvais was foaled. I haven't got the hang of the machine yet, so it's slow going. Particularly now that foaling season's almost here, and I'll have to post this year's births and matings regularly." Helen paused. "There may not be so many, though. We don't have as many mares in foal as usual, and two of our stud appointments were just canceled."

"That's too bad," I said absently. My mind was on the term paper I was about to start.

The morning routine around the stables was now in its winter pattern. Beginning while it was still dark, each horse was given breakfast—two quarts of mixed feed—and hosed down and brushed. It took about twenty minutes per horse, and I was now responsible for four, under Cyrus's eagle eye. After that Tom Beech came by, inspecting the animals carefully for injuries or signs of illness, a task at which he was particularly meticulous just now. Then the horses went out to pasture till early afternoon, and we stripped down the barns, washed them (also with particular care and disinfectant), and gave each stall new straw bedding.

After that I went back to the house and showered, and had a second breakfast with Rowena. And then, in proper office clothes—or at least in good pants and a sweater—I went out to the pine-paneled business office and worked on the computer. On the term papers, or on Rowena's records. The proper clothes were because I could be dealing with visitors or clients at any time, and because I felt like a part of management now. I loved the cozy office building, with its pine-paneled walls and furniture upholstered in dark green wool plaid, its glowing fire and horse photographs and trophies.

I was working in the main room alone one gray afternoon in the second week of January, when Rowena came out of her inner office, looking drawn.

"I just had a call. The insurance companies won't pay off the claim on the diseased stallion. He was absolutely clean when he left his former stable, and they've investigated every aspect of his journey south. They're convinced the bacteria was contracted here."

"Oh, Rowena." The phone rang imperiously, and I reached for it. "Unicorn Farm ... no, I'm sorry ... I'm sorry, but there's nothing I can tell you!" I banged the receiver down firmly.

"Who was that?" Rowena asked apprehensively.

"That same man who's called before, trying to locate Uncle Ned. He won't take no for an answer. Rowena, how *could* the bacteria be present here? None of the other horses have come down with it. You said it couldn't live except on animal matter, and the last case was over a year ago!"

"No, it wasn't," Rowena said. "It was in August. Bright Dancer. They sent specimens to the Center for Disease Control, and there were minute traces of the bacteria present. Thank God the bacteria doesn't affect humans, or we'd be on the verge of a full-scale disaster."

I nodded, my mind racing over what Rowena had said. "How could the bacteria have stayed virulent—I've seen the way everything here is disinfected! So how could Dancer have come down with it? Unless—"

I caught my breath.

"Go on," Rowena said, looking at me closely.

"I've been learning about diseases in that biology class I'm taking. We were talking about the way major epidemics have occurred; the Black Death centuries ago, and malaria, and typhoid. And AIDS. I kept thinking, there was a parallel between how AIDS is transmitted and what we know so far about the 'killer bacteria.' Only Dancer wasn't mated to a Unicorn Farm stallion, but to Secretariat. And Secretariat certainly doesn't have the bacteria! So that would mean—" I stopped uneasily.

"Say it," Rowena said steadily. "It's what's been going through my mind the past few weeks. It would mean the bacteria was transmitted, either by accident with an infected hypodermic needle, or deliberately."

We just looked at each other.

"Sarah," Rowena said very quietly, "I don't want you saying one word about this. Not to Tim, not to Gregory Stahl, not even to Cyrus or Tom Beech or Uncle Ned. To *no one*."

I nodded somberly.

The office was almost overly hot, but I felt a chill. Rowena shivered faintly, and moved toward the fireplace as though to poke the fire. She stopped midway, her gaze frozen on a photograph on the far wall.

My eyes followed hers to the picture of her parents smiling joyously beside Beauvais at the time of one of his early wins. The words Rowena had spoken to me the night she had first told me she suspected deliberate sabotage were suddenly ringing in my ears.

It means murder.

*R*umor must spread as fast as an epidemic. By late the next afternoon, five breeders had cabled or sent registered letters canceling their Unicorn Farm stud dates. Whether their stallions to our mares, or their mares to our stallions, didn't seem to matter. The horse world was scared.

"I can't blame them," Rowena said, drawing a deep breath. "If I suspected disease at another farm, I wouldn't breed with their stock, either."

"But there's no disease here now," I exclaimed.

"No, and there won't be," Rowena said. She got on the phone and hired a staff of security guards. We didn't refer again to the possibility of deliberate sabotage, but the suspicion hung in the air, mutually acknowledged.

Rowena also had an immunization crew recommended by Tim's professor come in and go over the entire stable area, as though they were searching for a bomb. She ordered blood tests for all the horses. Everything came up negative, and the public relations firm Rowena used took out full page ads

in all appropriate publications announcing the results of the findings.

As a result of all this, the rate of cancellations
slowed, but did not stop. "They're waiting to see if
any more horses die. And for the results of foaling
season," Tim said. True to my promise, I hadn't
discussed any of this with him, but he was tuned in
to the stable grapevine.

He didn't pump me even when he saw me close
to tears after another spate of letters canceling
Beau's stud dates arrived. I was touched, remem-
bering how he'd pushed me other times to confront
reality. Now he was bringing me bits of information
without comment, and I suspected he was respect-
ing my new status as part owner.

Tim drove me to take my exams, and when I
was finished with my work for the semester, he
advised me on courses to sign up for in the spring. I
chose another science class. He raised his eyebrows
when he saw that, but made no comment. Rowena's
comment was succinct: "The more both of us can
learn in that area, the better."

It was Tim who told me the trainers who hung
out around a local tavern were making book on
whether Rowena would be able to cover the first
payment on the million-plus loan she'd taken out to
buy the Saratoga stock.

"Including Luke Hoyle?" I demanded, shocked.

"Including Hoyle. No, I don't know which way
he's betting."

I didn't tell Rowena about the bets, but I did
probe delicately about the loan. "I don't know,"
Rowena said frankly. "We're hanging on by our
fingernails. I ought to make up a financial statement
for you and Uncle Ned. If I ever have time. Or if he

ever shows up. Oh, you've been working with the computer records! Look the figures up yourself." It was the first time she'd let her exhaustion show.

We were all exhausted, because foaling season had begun. Baby horses, like baby humans, were no respecters of the clock. "If we just do well in the breeding stall," Rowena said fervently, "healthy animals, no illnesses, a few promising colts . . . then maybe we'll be able to pick up the stud dates we lost."

"Greg hasn't canceled his bookings, has he?" I asked delicately. Greg had been conspicuous by his absence, now that I came to think of it. I'd been too engrossed to notice while exams were going on.

"Greg," Rowena said, "is back at Kitzbühel skiing."

But the gossip about Unicorn Farm troubles had crossed the ocean. The next day, which was bitter with sleet, an overnight registered letter with a Swiss stamp arrived at the business office. Rowena took it into her private sanctum to open it. I sat at the computer, my fingers jittery, until she buzzed me on the internal phone.

"Sarah, will you come in here a minute?"

I did so, my heart lurching. "Don't worry, he didn't cancel," she said when she saw my face. She held out the letter. "Shut the door and then read this."

My dearest Rowena,

This is a business offer, since you steadfastly refuse to listen when I have put these matters before you personally.
1. Will you marry me?

2. Will you sell Unicorn Farm, Inc. to Haseley Hall, Inc.? Offer is good for entire assets, *or* for equine stock only, *or* for real estate only (in which case, real estate would be available to you on perpetual lease, with rent to be waived for one year from the date of sale).

3. Will you agree to a business merger of the two firms?

4. Will you allow me to buy shares in ownership of Tapestry? (I do not suggest shares in Beauvais, since I know that is something you will not consider.)

> Your adoring and extremely anxious,
> Gregory

"At least he didn't mention anything about canceling his bookings," I said with more relevance than tact. And then, "What are you going to tell him?"

"Thanks but no thanks, to everything. With more graciousness than that, I do hope . . . He didn't say anything about *not* canceling, either, you notice."

"He'd hardly ask to buy into Tapestry if he thought there was a danger of bacteria. Love is one thing, a million-dollar investment is another, and Greg's a businessman." I eyed her. "It's none of my business, but how *do* you feel about him? Or should I say, why don't you marry him? Your feelings are pretty obvious."

"Are they?" Rowena asked a trifle grimly. "I couldn't marry him with this hanging over me. Maybe it's stubbornness. Maybe it's pride. I don't know . . . Sarah, I don't know *whom* I can trust now other than you and me."

That was the day I quietly decided to start an investigation of everyone whose life had interfaced with Unicorn Farm, beginning with the fire. Including Greg. Including even Tim.

I began it secretly, using the research techniques I'd been taught in my English lit class. Using the computer . . . there were so many statistics I'd been entering in it, names of employees, names of buyers, names of breeders. Pretending that I wanted to get the records updated before stud season, I pulled a couple of near all-nighters and finished entering data all the way back to the January first before the fire. Then I started pulling facts together, using a data management program, on some private computer disks of my own.

Armed with my lists of names, I invaded the college library. Finding information on Greg Stahl was easy; magazines and newspapers were constantly covering his doings. He had been in Lexington when the fire broke out; he had been the first to come to Rowena's aid. How had he known to come, and so quickly? I made a note to pump Rowena casually.

I was wading through piles of back magazines at a library table one afternoon, when Tim loomed over me. "Rowena thought you might be here. What are you doing? Not another term paper already!" Spring semester had only started the week before.

"Some research on owners of horses we're going to breed with," I answered, carefully casual. "I thought, since I'm keeping the breeding records, and don't know much about these people . . ." I left the sentence hanging.

"You're checking up on him, too, are you?" Tim said thoughtfully, looking over my shoulder. I was in the middle of reading an article in a two-year-old issue of *Town and Country*. "The New International Equine Entrepreneur," it was called, and it was about Greg Stahl.

"Nice little places he owns, aren't they?" Tim commented, looking at a photograph of Greg's home outside Geneva. Then his eyes moved on to photographs of Greg at New York racetracks, and I heard him draw his breath.

"What's the matter?" I asked at once.

"That's some company the guy keeps. One of those men he's shown with was indicted in Florida last year for fixing races, and the other was under suspicion in England for doping horses, but it was never proved."

"How do you know so much about those things?"

Tim looked at me. "I can read too."

I remembered that Rowena had sent Tim here, and asked him why. Tim said Rowena suspected Shining Star was going into labor. She wanted to stay with the mare, and wanted me personally to mind the phone.

He helped me gather up the magazines, suggesting that I check them out and take them with me. We drove back to the farm, and I found Rowena waiting impatiently in the business office. "Thank heaven!" she exclaimed as I entered. "Shining Star's been pacing at the back of her field since shortly after you left for class this morning. Cyrus is bringing her in to the foaling stall now. She may not deliver till late tonight, and I mean to stay with her. If you go up to the house, Sarah, switch the calls by call forwarding to the house line. If you're on the grounds, stay close enough to a phone so you can answer."

What she expected, or feared, I could not imagine, but one thing was clear: She wanted us to know about every call that came in.

Rowena hurried out toward the broodmare barn, and right after that I saw Cyrus through the window, leading Shining Star in for the night. The black Labrador, Shadow, trotted at their heels. Tim went off to study, and I settled down in the office with the phone and my magazines, entering tidbits of background information in the computer as I read.

Around six o'clock Tim returned with two steaming, foil-wrapped piepans. He'd made burgoo, his special stew. "I've brought your dinner. I just took Rowena hers."

"You're expecting me to eat for two?" I inquired innocently.

"Can't leave you to eat alone, can I?" Tim threw himself onto the plaid sofa and began digging into his burgoo with gusto. While we were eating, I took another of those mysterious phone calls for Dr. Drake.

After dinner I rang the broodmare barn and Rowena and we told each other that there was no news. "Except there was a call for Uncle Ned again," I added.

"Same person?" Rowena asked sharply.

"Same."

"I'm beginning to get worried myself," she said. Whether she was referring to Uncle Ned or the calls, I wasn't sure. "Close down the office whenever you want. You can switch calls to the house, and take them there. Or you can come here."

Like the other stable people, I kept a set of work clothes, an old windbreaker, and boots in a locker in the office building—a wing with locker rooms and showers had been added on in the general rebuilding after the fire. I changed and locked up the offices, and Tim walked me down the length of the stable area to the broodmare barn. An icy wind bit into our faces.

Inside the barn, though, everything was warm and peaceful. This was one of the oldest of the farm buildings, and it looked it. Bare light bulbs glowed on cords, and lanterns hung from heavy old iron hooks. A yellow cat washed herself in the doorway of the foaling stall.

Rowena and Cyrus were kneeling on the straw inside, on either side of the heaving mare. The white star blazed against the damp darkness of her forehead. This was not Shining Star's first colt, but she was clearly not thrilled with this stage of the proceedings.

"Tim, you go home," Rowena said, not looking up. And when he'd done so, "Sarah, lock the doors and then come here. In a few minutes or so I'm going to need you."

So Rowena had decided she, and I, and Cyrus, were to be the only midwives. It was the same as her saying we were the only three that she could trust.

Shining Star's contractions were stronger and closer together when I returned. I knelt down where Rowena told me to. And about fifteen minutes later the foal began to appear.

I'd seen the film on the birth of a racehorse that's shown regularly at the Kentucky Horse Farm Park, but this was different, because I was *there.* It felt so strange; it felt as if I were standing off a distance watching myself as I held one fragile front leg of the still-being-born foal, and Cyrus held the other. Rowena cradled the head, keeping it from drooping heavily on the delicate neck. There was a white blaze like its mother's on the dark forehead.

Shining Star gave one more mighty heave. The foal slid out and landed in a glistening heap on the straw. A little colt, by Beauvais out of Shining Star ... I looked at Rowena with a lump in my throat, and saw that Rowena's eyes, too, were wet.

Shining Star was already scrambling to her feet. Within minutes the colt was scrambling, too, comically. He rose on wide-spread, stiltlike legs, went down again as they collapsed beneath him. He gave us a look of outraged astonishment and tried again. On the third try he made it, though it took him several attempts to wobble around to his mother's side without banging against a wall. Rowena and I sat back on our heels and laughed till the tears ran down our faces.

Cyrus ran expert old hands over the colt as he nursed. "Good conformation and spirit. He's in good shape. Not a sign of trouble. You two go back to the house and get some sleep. I'll sack down here." He settled himself comfortably in two chairs across the entrance of the stall, the Labrador beside him.

Rowena and I, exhausted but elated, walked back to the house. As we approached the back door, Rowena frowned.

"There's a light on. Were you in here this afternoon?" I shook my head, and she pursed her lips. "I could swear I hadn't left one on."

We let ourselves in cautiously. The door had been locked, but a heavy odor of tobacco permeated the kitchen. A dirty plate, cup, and saucer sat

on the drainboard, and a few minutes later a stento-
rian voice came trumpeting down the backstairs.

"Doesn't anyone believe in keeping regular meal
hours if I'm not here?"

The wandering Dr. Drake had returned.

*T*he next day Rowena registered the colt with the Jockey Club's thoroughbred registry. She turned to me as she filled out the forms. "This is the first colt you've helped deliver, the first colt you've seen born. And the first at Unicorn Farm since you've become part owner. What would *you* like to name it?"

I remembered the first sight of the small dark head with its inquisitive eyes and the blaze just like his mother's. "Starfire," I said softly.

Starfire by Beauvais out of Shining Star. Alive, healthy, definitely kicking when we took him outdoors with his mother on the second morning of his life. His birth seemed a good omen.

Two days later Shining Star was dead. There was no apparent reason. She simply died.

"It's not the bacteria! She showed none of the symptoms," Rowena cried fiercely, fighting back tears. She ordered an immediate autopsy.

A few days later another mare was brought to the foaling stall and delivered a stillborn colt. Dr.

Voelkner, when summoned, could find no apparent cause and advised an autopsy in this case also. That night, waking in the small hours and unable to fall back asleep, I heard footsteps going quietly down the stairs. After a short while I followed. A fan of light poured through the study doorway in the darkened hall.

I found Rowena at her desk, her head on one hand, poring over papers. She looked up with a sad smile as I went in. "Oh, Sarah. I thought I was doing something good for you, bringing you here. I thought giving you shares would help you feel it was your home. It looks like I've only heaped more troubles on you."

"Don't say that." I went around and hugged her. "I'm *family!* And I'm strong. So are you. Good grief, haven't we proved that enough already? Whatever happens, we can face it together, and we'll survive."

"I've been facing one thing already," Rowena said simply. "If the income projected for February doesn't materialize, I'll have to sell Starfire. I'm sorry, Sarah."

"Don't think about that yet!" A thought struck me. "Or think about this. You said there's enough money from Mother's insurance to send me for four years to a good college. Let me buy Starfire with it. I don't want to go away to college anyway; I want to stay here. Being a day student at the university won't cost so much."

Rowena started to shake her head, then saw the look in my eyes. "We'll cross that bridge when we have to," she temporized. "What I'm mainly worried about right now is that loan payment."

"Did anything else happen today beside that colt being born dead?"

Rowena nodded. "You know we have some mares being boarded here from out-of-state till their foals are delivered and they're mated again to Unicorn stallions? I've been half-expecting some of those stud appointments to be canceled, but at least we could count on the boarding and delivery fees. This afternoon two owners notified me they're transferring the mares to other Lexington farms first thing tomorrow. They don't want to risk something happening to the animals here during birthing."

We looked at each other. "How do you think the news traveled this time?" I asked. "I thought the crew was supposed to keep their mouths shut!"

"To keep their mouths shut about the bacteria, and they're mostly going along on that because they're afraid if they lose these jobs, they won't find others easily after working here. The foaling deaths are different. There wasn't any carelessness; there wasn't any disease. It just happened out of the blue."

"Don't say it. The Unicorn Farm curse strikes again!" I snorted. "That Luke! I'll bet you anything he's the one who talked! I just don't trust him."

"Trainers are free agents, and good ones are in enough demand that they don't feel loyalty unless it's been earned. I agree Luke's a very rough diamond, but he knows his job. At least," Rowena said frankly, "we don't have to worry about the leak being Uncle Ned. He's been keeping very close to home ever since he got back."

I wished he hadn't come back, but I couldn't say so. His low profile did not extend to keeping out of stable business. He now felt more free than ever to push his nose into it.

During that next week the two pregnant mares

were picked up for transport to other farms. Another mare who was being boarded came to term on a day of drizzling rain. She had an agonizingly protracted labor, and Dr. Voelkner, reached by phone but busy with a patient elsewhere, prescribed a muscle relaxant. Luke himself drove into town to make the purchase. Uncle Ned supervised the measuring of the dose, which K.T. administered. The filly was finally born two hours later, but was weak and breathed with difficulty.

Within the hour she, too, was dead.

Rowena rose stiffly from the straw. "Sarah, I want you to walk the mare into a stall in the other broodmare barn. All the rest of you, please leave. I want to see you in my office at ten tomorrow."

When I returned from bedding down the mare, I found the other barn locked up and a security guard at the door.

Rowena had left everything in the foaling stall just as it was, and she had Dr. Voelkner there making a careful examination of the evidence by sunup. *Evidence* . . . the word, flashing into my mind, brought me up short. I was already thinking of this as a crime. I couldn't help myself.

The meeting in Rowena's office was grim. It consisted of Rowena and myself, Dr. Voelkner, and those who had been involved in the birth or in caring for the mare. Uncle Ned, K.T., and Luke Hoyle; Tom Beech and Cyrus and Tim and another stablehand.

"From a cursory examination, I'd say the mare probably took a chill," Dr. Voelkner said, and took everyone through the circumstances of the past three days. The temperature in the barn had been maintained; Tim and the other stablehand confirmed each other on that. The mare had been fed exactly what she was supposed to eat.

"*He* can back that up," the stablehand said acidly, jerking his head at Luke. Luke, officially a trainer, had been interpreting his job to include strict supervision of all feeding. Since this was keeping the feed bill down, Rowena let him get away with it, provided he didn't interfere with Beau.

The injection of muscle relaxant was discussed. K.T. produced the bottle, which Dr. Voelkner pocketed for checking. Uncle Ned cleared his throat. "I can vouch for proper dosage," he said grandly. "Although it was somewhat higher than I'd have recommended. I measured it out in a sterile container in front of all these persons, and supervised its induction into a hypodermic newly removed from its sealed wrapper."

"I looked at the measurements on the vial," Tim said quietly. "They were exactly what they were supposed to be." Dr. Drake threw him a suspicious glance and rumbled an ungracious thanks.

They proceeded to the mare's routine the day before. "I took her out to her regular paddock at seven, as Mr. Hoyle told me to," Tim said.

Luke sat up straight. "I told you to keep her in till the sun was full up! If that raw rain kept up, I didn't want her out at all!" He swung on Rowena angrily. "The doctor says the mare took a chill? There's your reason! I'm fed up with this smart-aleck kid acting like he's got some kind of inside knowledge instead of doing what he's told. You'd think he was related to you too," he added with a glance of dislike in my direction. Dr. Drake shot a sharp look from Luke to Tim, who was staring at his feet. Luke stood up, banging his fist down on Rowena's desk.

"I told the kid to take the mare out at nine, if at all, and he disobeyed, and now you have a fatality on your hands. And if you can't pick and control your help better than this, Miss Drake, you have no business trying to run a horse farm."

"I did what you told me to," Tim said doggedly.

Luke's eyes blazed. "Are you calling me a liar?"

"Stop it, all of you." Rowena's tone was icy. "Actually, Hoyle, it was not your place, either, to decide whether the mare should have been taken out. That was up to me or Mr. Beech." Her precise usage of their names was pointed. "Tim, have you anything more to say?" He shook his head. "Then you may all leave."

Anyone who could say Rowena was not in command, and did not know how to use authority properly, I thought, was crazy.

I had a class that afternoon, and I went, because I thought my staying home would make Rowena worry about my being worried. Actually I was, and deeply. Tim drove me to class, and neither of us spoke much. "Why didn't you defend yourself more?" I asked once, and he shrugged.

"People like Hoyle believe only what they want to. Or maybe they act the way they want you to think they believe. Maybe I'm way out of line, but I don't think it was the mare's being out in the rain yesterday that caused the foal's death."

"So you're an expert on mares and foals too?" I teased gently. Tim didn't answer. I shot a glance at him and was surprised to find his lips pressed tight. "Tim? You *have* been around breeding operations a lot, haven't you?"

"Not enough to know why that foal died," Tim said.

For some reason, that exchange—and the way he'd behaved in the office, and what Luke had said there—hung in my memory.

Tim was in a class when my class got out, and I started walking home through a depressing drizzle. I was trudging along Ironworks Pike lost in thought, when a small van coming from the other direction hailed me. It was K.T. "Come on, I'll give you a ride."

"You're on your way home."

"That's all right, I don't mind going out of my way." She swung the van around on the slippery road, and I climbed in. "Some scene this morning," she commented.

"Some scene Luke Hoyle made. Sorry, I forgot you liked him."

"You can be hooked on somebody without liking them," K.T. said soberly. It was a strange thing for her to say. I looked at her, startled, but her face was blank.

I reached the house to find a family argument going on in the front parlor. Or it would have been an argument if Rowena had picked up the bait; right then it was one-sided, with the sound and fury coming from Uncle Ned. "Damn all, girl! You'd be out of all this mess if you'd listen to reason! Syndication's the only way to go. We'd all be millionaires then, curse or no curse! But no!" He swung a disparaging arm around, indicating the Victorian perfection of the room. "Why in hell do you have to keep this place in the nineteenth century just because your father was short-sighted? And for that matter, why don't you marry that foreigner and raise some kids in a life of ease instead of diverting all your female instincts to a herd of horses?"

If I was Rowena, I'd have struck him. What Rowena did was say coldly, "You're the one who's trying to turn the clock back to a time that's gone, aren't you, Ned? You're never going to have a second chance at college days."

The ambiguous statement shut him up completely. He flung himself off. "What was that about?" I asked, stepping in from the hall.

"It's not important. Come into the study, will you? I have to make a business phone call, and I want a witness." Rowena's face was pale, and her voice controlled. I followed her, wondering, and I wondered more when she gave the overseas operator a Swiss telephone number and instructed her to locate Mr. Gregory Stahl and ring back when she had done so.

"*Business* call?" I asked.

"Business." Rowena ran her fingers through her hair. "I just heard from the insurance company. No, not about the bacteria," she added quickly. "About Shining Star, and the filly that just died. The insurance company will pay on that coverage. But then they're canceling my policy unless I agree to a high-risk rate that will cost three times as much. And they won't cover further births at all until the cause of the two most recent deaths is settled."

"Dear God," I said slowly.

The telephone rang, and Rowena picked it up. "Yes ... Then keep trying to locate him." She hurriedly found Greg's Geneva phone number for the operator. "Someone on staff there should know other numbers you can try.... Yes, bill all calls to this number." She dropped the receiver in its cradle and turned back. "Sarah, do you have your checkbook with you?"

I was startled. "Yes, it's in my purse."

"Write a check to Unicorn Farms, Inc., for five hundred dollars. I'm selling you Starfire. And I've just bought Beau back from the corporation. I won't go into a long legal explanation, but the basic facts are that Unicorn Farms, Inc., owns the breeding stock, the breeding and boarding operations, and all the equipment that's involved. It also owns the horses I bought at Saratoga, and is responsible for those loans. If the loan payments can't be met, or if there are any more—accidents, and the insurance company won't make good on them, it's the corporation that will be sued, not you or me or Ned. We may lose the business, but you won't lose Starfire. And I won't lose Beau, or the manor house. That doesn't belong to the corporation, only the stable buildings and paddocks do."

I stared at her. "You don't think it will possibly come to that!"

"I don't know what to think," Rowena said simply. "Maybe I ought to—"

The phone rang again, and she grabbed it.

"Greg," I heard her say in a voice that was half a laugh and half a sigh. Then I could feel her willing herself back in control. "No . . . no, I can't. Not now . . . Greg, please, just listen." She stopped briefly, collected herself, and went on calmly. "You were willing to buy shares of Tapestry if I'd syndicate him. I won't do that, but will you buy him outright? We've had more problems. No, not the bacteria, but the insurance judgment on that went against us. There's been one foal born dead, and another died shortly after. And two days after her delivery, Shin-

ing Star died. We don't know why. My insurance rate just skyrocketed, and my loan payment's due."

She was silent, listening, as a myriad of emotions went across her face. "Yes, that will do beautifully . . . Greg, *no*. You needn't . . . Very well, then. The day after tomorrow."

She put down the phone, looking exhausted but relieved. "He's going to phone his attorney here immediately. The papers will be brought tonight for signing, and the funds will be transferred when the banks open up tomorrow. And he insists on flying back here the next day."

That did not surprise me. Nothing that had happened since the first of the year surprised me. Maybe I was getting fatalistic. Maybe I was simply getting numb. Not the numbness of avoiding feelings, but a different kind of calmness, deep within. It was as if I'd looked at what life had dished out to me squarely in the face, and paid the cost, and now my emotions were skin-deep only.

Rowena's hand was caressing the small brass unicorn standing on the desk. Catching my look, she smiled. "Do you know what this is? Dad gave me this as a trophy after Beau's fall in the Derby. He said even if I never raced again, or Beau never did, we were both champions, and unique. Like unicorns; like Unicorn Farm. That loving horses, loving this piece of land, was a fever in the blood. That that could be a blessing or a curse, like a two-edged sword . . ." She laughed slightly.

Rowena had said she didn't know what to think. I knew what I thought. It simply couldn't be coincidence that so many things were going wrong. It couldn't be mismanagement, because with her years of work Rowena couldn't be that poor a manager.

And Tom Beech, Dr. Voelkner, K.T. despite her youth, even Luke Hoyle—all of them had excellent professional reputations. If Dr. Drake had been calling the shots on the equine maternity ward, that would have been something else, I thought—and brought myself up short.

How much did I really know about Uncle Ned? I'd told him about those phone calls while he was away. He'd cross-examined me, then become truculent and wary. How much—like his not drinking since the stallion died—was I taking just on hearsay? And how much *did* I know about all those people?

Not much—not even about Tim. I was a newcomer, in a world to which the others had belonged for generations. And I'd let myself get sidetracked from my research by the catastrophes of the past week.

Instead of going upstairs and changing, I put my coat back on and went around to the business office, where I'd left the library magazines. The pile was smaller than I'd remembered, and when I had them back in my bedroom and was flipping through them, I frowned. Then, because the business office was already closed for the day, I buzzed Rowena.

"I brought a pile of magazines home from the library the day Starfire was born. I left them in the office, and some of them are gone. I know, because I just looked for an article on the Derby that I'd been reading. Did you take them?"

Rowena laughed slightly. "When have I had time to read? No, you left some of the magazines in Tim's car. He dropped them here at the house the next day, and I forgot to tell you. They're in the upstairs hall."

I went out to the small sitting area Rowena called a foyer, located between her bedroom and Uncle Ned's. The magazines were there, piled haphazardly on the coffee table. I scooped them up and carried them back to my room.

I started flipping through them, looking at pictures and stories at random. And then I stopped. In the center of one of the major racing magazines, several pages had been ripped out. Roughly, as though in haste.

Something, some intuition I hadn't known I had, told me the subject of the missing article even before I located the title on the contents page.

It was an in-depth feature report on the Unicorn Farm fire.

*T*he fire. It all came back to that, didn't it?

Rowena thought the fire had been deliberate. But it couldn't have been, could it? Because nothing up till then, so far as I knew, had warranted so terrible a thing.

So far as I knew.

What could be the motives for arson, I wondered, thinking hard. *Revenge.* (But for what?) *Greed.* (Who needed money that bad? More to the point, who if anyone had profited from the fire?) *Malice.* (Why?) *Rivalry.* (Did I really believe a competing horse breeder would resort to arson?)

I was frustrated, and I was restless. I put my outer things back on and, calling out to Rowena that I was going out back and would return to help with dinner, I went to the business office. I locked myself in, and I started hacking through my computer files, looking for possible motives in the records of the months before the fire.

Nobody had been let go. There had been no catastrophes. I even, feeling more than a little ashamed, rooted around for the year's bookkeeping records. Unicorn Farm had been turning a healthy profit. No, I thought, Rowena had been wrong. If there was some kind of malignancy, like a cancer, spreading its tentacles through the world of Unicorn Farm, the fire had not been the result of it. It had been its cause.

I went back to the house and, after dinner, devoured those magazines. The next day I tried to get another copy of the one with the missing pages from the library, but with no luck. Then I had an idea. That afternoon I asked a woman in my psych class who commuted to college from Louisville if she'd get me a copy of the magazine from the library there. She was a pleasant married woman in her thirties, also a part-timer, and uncurious. She said she would.

Greg was at the manor house when I returned that afternoon. He was again in the parlor with Rowena, and I could tell from the expression on their faces when I walked in that he had again been proposing.

"I couldn't say yes with all that's hanging over us," she confided later.

"And afterward?" I asked, having a feeling I'd asked the question once before.

"Afterward . . . we'll see."

I was relieved, because I was beginning to feel uneasy. My magazine reading had pointed up the playboy side of Greg, and it had also made clear that the big-money aspects of the horse business included high-stakes gambling. Greg Stahl socialized with those gamblers at casinos and racetracks, perhaps did business with them. How could that have a connection with Unicorn Farm? I didn't know, but it started my wheels turning.

The security corps had been augmented, since the foal deaths, by a closed-circuit TV surveillance network. There were cameras in all the stalls, in the breeding barn, and around the grounds. Now we would know at once if anyone was, as the doctor expressed it, "attempting hanky-panky."

We were in the middle of the stud season now. Forget about romance, I thought after witnessing my first such encounters through the glass viewing window in the breeding barn. Thoroughbred breeding was big business and high science. It was also a swift routine. Despite the cancellation of stud appointments, we still had a full schedule, what with our own mares, the mares sent in for mating (judicious spreading of the news that we now had augmented insurance coverage kept this happening), and the mares and stallions sent over from Haseley Hall.

Breeding started at five-thirty in the morning and went on, at twenty-minute intervals, for three hours, with another three hours scheduled in the afternoons. The actual rendezvous of mare and stallion took a fast four minutes; the rest of the time was devoted to a hospitallike washing down of the barn and everything, animate or inanimate, it would contain. All this was supervised by scientists from the university school of equine diseases. Rowena was taking no chances with either bacteria or rumors of bacteria.

Beauvais was kept very busy, and so was Tapestry, whom Greg was boarding at Unicorn Farm for the duration. Whether he was doing this to demonstrate his faith in the farm's clean bill of health, or because he didn't want to risk Tapestry's carrying the bacteria to Haseley Hall, I didn't know, and I knew better than to ask. In any event, both Beauvais and Tapestry were blooming with health and hormones.

"We should have a good season with foals this coming year, God willing," Rowena said prayerfully.

Early spring was just touching the rolling fields with beauty when Tim's professor, Dr. Lang, drove into the stable yard one afternoon as Tim and I were coming in from a ride. "Where's Miss Drake?" he asked and, when I pointed at the office, went that way unsmiling. Tim and I looked at each other and followed.

Rowena's office door was shut, but shortly afterward she buzzed Helen Gallagher. Helen looked at us. "Round up Cyrus and Luke Hoyle, will you? And K.T.'s in the exercise barn, isn't she? I'll call her and Mr. Beech. And Dr. Drake. Miss D wants all of you in the office in five minutes."

The results of the autopsies on Shining Star, on the stillborn foal, and on the foal who had died soon after birth were in, and the professor minced no words. There were unexplained puncture marks on Shining Star, suggesting a drug had been given although no trace remained. "The deaths of both foals," he finished, "were definitely caused by drugs."

When the professor stopped speaking, there was a deadly silence. Then Dr. Drake and Mr. Beech both spoke at once.

"Damn all, there was only one drug administered, and I measured it! It was given to the mother, and in proper dosage!"

"The foals were never given any medication!"

The professor eyed them both to silence. "The

medication was the one Dr. Drake refers to, but in a much more highly concentrated formulation."

And it hadn't been prescribed in the first birth at all. The thought was almost visible in everybody's mind. Dr. Drake, I noticed, looked gray beneath his habitual purple.

"Dr. Drake's right," Tim said clearly. "He measured out exactly what the vet prescribed."

"And I kept the bottle afterward," Rowena said. "Locked in my safe."

The professor nodded. "Who picked up the medication?"

One after another we turned our eyes toward Luke Hoyle. And his cool broke. Not outwardly; on the inside, which was much more dangerous. All that showed was a little muscle flickering at the corner of his left eye. "You're not going to pin this on me," he said coldly. "I picked it up where I was told to, and I delivered it as I was told to. Sealed!" He appealed to Uncle Ned, who nodded. "I came to this cursed place as a favor to Mr. Gregory Stahl, and he can stuff it! I've had nothing to do with the mismanagement of Unicorn Farm, and I'm not going to spend any more time trying to shape up a hobby run by a bunch of women!"

K.T. made an involuntary sound. He swung on her, his eyes narrowing. "You gave the shot! What did you do, miss the target and shoot the stuff into the foal instead? Or did you supplement the dosage? Nobody measured the remaining contents of the bottle, as I recall!"

The virulence of his attack, of his voice, took my breath away. K.T. just sat there, stunned. It was Rowena who spoke.

"That's enough, Hoyle," she said icily. "Your services are terminated as of now. I expect you out of your quarters in an hour."

Luke Hoyle shot up, stood for a moment irresolute, then stomped out.

With his exit the tension burst like a balloon. "I think this has been quite enough for now," Rowena said. "There will be further investigation, naturally. Particularly into the deaths of Shining Star and the stillborn foal. In the light of these findings, I'm afraid the police must be brought in. I'll expect you all to cooperate with them fully. K.T., please stay. You, too, Sarah. The rest may leave."

But K.T., holding herself stiffly as if afraid she'd break, said she couldn't stay.

"I'll look for her in a little while," I told Rowena. When I did so, K.T.'s car was gone.

Rowena invited herself to dinner at Haseley Hall that night. I was with Tim, and our cooking session did not have its usual sparkle.

"I never did trust the guy," Tim said frankly, referring to Luke. "He's too smooth."

"You mean conceited!"

"That too. But it's more than that. He's like one of those gunfighters in old westerns."

"You think he's a hired gun?" I asked the question facetiously, but somehow or other the words came out with more weight than I'd intended. Tim's eyes narrowed.

"What made you think of that?"

"I don't know. His arrogance, I suppose. And the fact that he was hired by international high-flier Gregory Stahl. Tim, do you think any of this has any connection with racetrack gambling?"

Tim's eyes became alert. "What are you thinking? Don't pretend that you don't know."

"I don't, honestly. Except that horse racing has gambling, horse breeding's a gamble, and Greg knows gamblers. Maybe it's gambling, not the Unicorn fire, that's the cause of our catastrophes."

Tim wanted to know what I meant, and I told him my conviction that all the troubles stemmed from the fire. "I've been trying to dig up motives. Revenge. Greed. Don't laugh; maybe there's some connection between our stud and an international gambling syndicate."

"It would have to be international," Tim said. As I frowned, he laughed. "Sorry! Just thinking out loud. Maybe we've both been seeing too many movies. Exactly whose motives have you been looking into?"

"Everyone who was connected with the farm at the time of, or just before, the fire." I looked at him. "At least that frees you from suspicion! But . . . I feel awful; I catch myself wondering about everyone else. Even Cyrus! Even Uncle Ned."

"He's the logical one where the medication's concerned," Tim pointed out.

"Yes, if he wasn't so afraid of giving hypodermics! Anyway, he's had nothing to gain. He had no reason to think Rowena would ever give him even nonvoting ownership. He'd been disinherited long before. I'd love to know why." Then I caught the expression flitting across his face. *"Tim!"*

"Just rumors, that's all I've heard," Tim said quickly. "Most of them resentful. You know he's not exactly liked around the bunkhouse. If you want the reason, why haven't you asked Rowena?"

"I did, once. She said she didn't know."

"You could ask Cyrus. He's been here since Rowena's grandfather's day, hasn't he?" Tim asked.

I did not tell Rowena about this conversation, nor did I tell her about my fishing expedition with Cyrus the following afternoon. I found him feeding Beauvais oats and honey after Beau's matrimonial exertions, and started to ask questions about Beau's bloodlines. Then I led him back into reminiscences of Unicorn Farm in an earlier day. Some were interminable, some brought a lump to my throat, but I persevered. At last we got into the days when Uncle Ned and Uncle Gil were boys together.

"They must have loved it here," I said artfully. "You can see from the way Dr. Drake keeps coming back here still, even though he has that apartment in New York."

Cyrus looked at me through bland old eyes, and I had a feeling he was seeing straight through me. He said merely, "Yep," in a way that indicated he could speak volumes.

"I suppose he was all wrapped up in medicine, though, once he'd gone to college. Is that why his father decided to make Uncle Gil his heir, because Uncle Gil studied animal husbandry and kept on working here?"

Cy sat down on the bench outside Beau's stall and scratched Shadow's head between the ears. After a minute he went on, in that casual, reminiscent tone. "Old Mr. Drake cut Mr. Ned out because of the carousing Mr. Ned did at Duke. Because he got drunk on juleps or those fancy cocktails folks drank then, and lost Gobelins in a gambling bet. Gobelins was one of Mr. Drake's prize stallions, what he'd given Mr. Ned as a twenty-first birthday gift."

He said it offhand, not looking at me, as if he

didn't know exactly what he was doing or why I had been asking.

I went back to the manor house with my brain whirling. Drink, and Uncle Ned. Malpractice, and Uncle Ned. Uncle Ned falling off the wagon . . . around the time of the fire? I wondered, breathing hard. Uncle Ned making a public spectacle of his unwillingness to administer hypodermics. Uncle Ned involved with gambling.

All at once I was running, afraid of my own thoughts. It could not be true. Uncle Ned could not be doing all this—this evil, to Rowena. Yet who else had a motive . . . unless I could find a way to link the fire with Gregory Stahl.

Which would Rowena rather lose, Greg or her uncle?

I ran into the house, and up the stairs, avoiding contact with Rowena. In my own room, I locked the door and began frantically, feverishly, thumbing through those magazines, my notes, my computer printouts. All for nothing.

Damn that missing article about the fire! I thought.

I walked into psych class the next day and my friend hailed me with a smile. "I found what you wanted."

I thrust the magazine into my notebook, and when class was done I went, not to the college library, not back to Unicorn Farm, but downtown. I caught a bus downtown, and went into a coffee shop where I'd never been before, and ordered coffee and a Kentucky melt before taking out the magazine.

Something must have been telling me I'd need to

be with people who were strangers, the better to hold myself together. Because when I opened the magazine to the article about the Unicorn fire, one of the first things I saw, after photographs of the terrible devastation, was a photo spread of people who had suffered bad losses in the fire.

There was Rowena, her face a mask of tragedy, in front of the ruins in which her parents had died. The next picture was of an elderly man in rumpled suit and glasses: *Mr. Simon Atkins of Tallahassee, Florida, whose stakes winner, Tagalog, boarding at Unicorn Farm in training for the Derby, died in the fire. Shown at the Florida races on a happier occasion.*

The figure directly behind Mr. Atkins, sharing his program and laughing, was Tim Payne.

I got myself home from the coffee shop in a taxi. We drove through the gates of Unicorn Farm after they'd been opened by a security guard, and up the drive beneath trees beginning to show a tender green. Mares and foals, including Starfire, gamboled in the paddocks. Somewhere out back Beau would be running, reveling in the spring sunlight. Tapestry would be running too. On the exercise track; Greg was planning to enter him in the April races at the Keeneland track. Then, if he did well, the Wood Memorial or the Blue Grass Stakes; perhaps the Derby.

It would be a credit to Rowena, even more than to Greg, if he won. Tapestry was a Unicorn Farm stallion, born and bred; his being sold to Haseley Hall couldn't change that. No more horses had died. There had been no more signs of the killer bacteria. Maybe, just maybe, Unicorn Farm was entering an upswing. I should have been glad. Instead, all I was thinking was that the farm was like an armed camp on terrorist alert. And maybe the terrorist was inside.

I didn't go out back that afternoon. I was so quiet during dinner that Rowena asked me if I had a headache. I mumbled an excuse. That night, and all the next morning, which was Saturday, I shut myself in my room and pored over my magazines.

There wasn't anything in them identifying Tim, but there were two paragraphs about Simon Atkins. He was a retired Florida orange grower who kept a few horses and had bought one of Unicorn Farm's yearlings for the fun of it. An expensive hobby, but it had looked like it was going to be self-supporting because the colt, by the time he was a three-year-old, showed great promise. He'd boarded it at Unicorn Farm for training, and it had won the Blue Grass Stakes. It had been entered in the Derby. It had died in the fire.

There was the motive for revenge. The article said the insurance policies had not been sufficient to cover all the owners' losses.

Rowena wasn't home that day. If I remembered correctly, she was visiting her lawyer's and insurance agent's offices before going to Haseley Hall for a business conference with Greg. He wanted Tapestry to stay at Unicorn Farm for the duration of spring training, but he also wanted Luke Hoyle to conduct that training, which certainly did not go down well with Rowena. In addition, Rowena and Greg were jointly plotting strategy to make sure Unicorn Farm's bill of health was squeaky clean in time for the racing season.

All that meant Rowena would not be home again for some time. I had the house to myself. I was about to make some phone calls, when it occurred to me that Uncle Ned was probably up in his third-floor study. He spent most of his time up there these days. I wouldn't want to risk his listening in. Not that he was likely to, I thought; the fight had all gone out of him these days.

I was spared from concocting an excuse for checking on him. The phone rang. I answered. It was one of those male strangers, a different one this time, asking for Dr. Drake. "He may be here. I'll check," I said briefly. I punched the hold button and climbed the stairs to the third floor.

I'd never been in Uncle Ned's study, and its door was closed now. I knocked, and his hoarse voice said, "Who is it?"

"It's Sarah." I didn't have a chance to say why I was there, because he interrupted with a sharp "Just a minute," and I heard objects being scrabbled. Then the latch was thrown, and the door opened just enough to reveal his figure, more disheveled if possible than usual.

I gave my message, and his eyes bulged. "No, I'm busy! Don't say that, tell them I'm not here!" He banged the door.

I went downstairs, picked up the phone in the foyer, and relayed this misinformation, adding that I had no idea when the doctor would return.

When I put down the phone and turned around, I saw Uncle Ned standing at the top of the stairs, listening. For a minute our eyes met, and he reddened and turned away. "Wait!" I called impulsively, and ran halfway up the stairs. Then I stopped, and composed my words carefully.

Uncle Ned . . . would you tell me what you remember about the fire? I can't ask Rowena, because thinking about it makes her feel so bad. But I need to know everything I can, so I'll understand.

I'll put my foot in my mouth without meaning to, otherwise."

"I don't know a damn thing more than she's told me, either," Dr. Drake said truculently. "It happened when I was in my second residence at a rest home. Euphemism for drying-out tank, for which I have already given you an accounting." Instead of going back to his study, he stomped downstairs out of doors, leaving me with privacy to make my phone calls.

I called K.T. first, ostensibly to ask her how she was. "I'm fine," she said in a guarded voice. Then, after a pause, "Why am I trying to kid you? I hurt like hell. Mainly in self-esteem."

"You don't have to worry about anybody believing those things Luke said. We know you had no reason to tamper with the medication." *None that we've found so far,* a voice added in my head.

"Thanks for that." K.T. was silent for a moment. "You know what hurts most? Not the fact that Luke suspects me. I don't even think he does. I was just somebody convenient he could put the blame on, to take suspicion off himself! And I'd been gullible enough—me!—to think he was seriously interested in me. That's the worst part. I fell for him, and all he was interested in, probably, was the information he could pump out of me!"

"What information?" I asked quickly.

"Oh, anything he could find out about Unicorn Farm. I thought it was because he was interested in me, in my work. He was probably here as an industrial spy—if you can conceive of such a thing in the horse breeding industry." She laughed without humor.

"I suppose it's easy for people to get work on

the horse farms under false pretenses. Or with false credentials," I said through dry lips.

"Not that easy. It's a small world, and references are taken seriously. I was being unfair; Luke Hoyle is an accredited trainer, and a good one, in spite of being a mean maverick. He'd have to be for Gregory Stahl to have hired him for Miss D in the first place." So K.T. knew about that, I reflected. Then she laughed again, a real laugh this time. "Don't you worry, Sarah. *Tim's* a genuine thoroughbred, in all senses."

"Do you . . . know anything about him?"

"Nothing more than I can see with my own eyes. He's crazy about you, as if you didn't know."

I put down the phone. The headache Rowena had accused me of having last night was becoming real. I stood for several minutes, irresolute, and then I took out the phone book, looked up the Tallahassee area code, and called information there for the number of Simon Atkins.

The operator told me the number had been disconnected.

All at once I was feeling suffocatingly hot. The ticking of the clock in the lower hall sounded like a bomb. Air, that was what I needed. Air, and exercise. I went out back, and skirting carefully around barns while checking their interiors through the windows, I saddled Jeeter and rode toward the far end of Unicorn Farm's back five hundred acres.

As soon as I was out of sight of the barns I began to gallop. I rode till my muscles were sore, but that didn't stop the soreness inside. At last I found myself behind the back end of Beauvais's paddock, and dismounted, tying Jeeter's reins loosely to a fence rail. Jeeter nibbled grass quietly. Beau spotted me and approached skittishly, acting coy and flirting. I climbed onto the top rail and hugged him, burying my face in his mane. Beau nuzzled me and, his eye on the main chance, searched my pockets. I fed him peppermints. Then I closed my eyes and just drooped as the thing I didn't want to face grew bigger and bigger till it was like a billboard behind my eyes.

Who had been hurt badly enough by the fire to want to sabotage Unicorn Farm? Simon Atkins, for one.

Beau's rough tongue rasped the back of my neck, and I jerked away.

"I could do better than that," Tim's voice said behind me, only half-amused.

"What do you want?" I asked in a muffled voice, not turning.

"To find out what's eating you. You've been avoiding me all yesterday and today, and I want to know why." I didn't answer, and he came up close and began to rub my shoulders.

I couldn't help myself; I flinched.

"Something's happened," Tim said in a completely altered voice. He jumped up beside me and turned me forcibly to face him. "I thought we were through being on guard with each other."

"Ha!"

"What does that mean?" Tim asked evenly.

"It means I know about Mr. Simon Atkins!"

I don't know what I expected—that he'd look bewildered, that he'd deny knowing the name. What I didn't expect was that after a long minute he'd say, with a sigh of relief, "I'm glad. It's been driving me crazy not being able to tell you."

"Tell me what? That you're the curse of Unicorn

Farm?" I started to laugh, hiccuping. "K.T.'s right.
It's discovering your own gullibility that hurts the
most!"

"What on earth are you talking about?" Tim
asked in complete mystification. "I thought you meant
you'd found out Simon Atkins was my grandfather."

"And that's why you came here pretending to be
just a college kid from New York State. So you
could ... get revenge on Unicorn Farm for your
grandfather's losses in the fire."

"If you believe that, you're the one who's crazy,"
Tim said flatly. "And I don't think revenge has anything to do with the curse on Unicorn Farm. Look,
do we have to talk here? I'll get a horse, and we can
ride somewhere private."

He did so. We rode to the far back reaches of
the property, hobbled our mounts, and sat down
beneath a tree.

"All right," Tim said. "I'll talk. You listen."

"You sound like Luke Hoyle."

"Don't drag him into it. Or maybe he *is* in it. I'll
get to that. The main point," Tim said, his voice
growing quiet, "is that Simon Atkins was my grandfather, and I loved him very much."

"Past tense?"

"Past tense. He died the day after Christmas."
His eyes flicked toward me briefly. "That's why I
left New York early. I do live there, by the way. The
family flew to Florida for the funeral, and then I—I
just needed to get back here. And I needed you."

I made a small involuntary gesture toward him,
and he said, "No. Not till I get this all out first. It's
important that I do." He pulled one leg up and
hooked his arms around his knee, and I waited.

"I always spent as much vacation time as my

folks would let me, down at Gramps's. Ever since I was a kid. He's why I ended up studying horse management. And I'm why he bought Tagalog. 'Tagalog out of Cluny II by Beauvais.' Gramps hoped to make enough money racing him to help with my grad school, and then he and I would use Tag to start our stud. He loved that horse."

A chilly breeze stirred my hair. I did not move.

"I didn't know it, but Gramps, like a darn fool, had taken out a second mortgage on the orange groves to finance Tag. He'd worked hard all his life, he was in his seventies and a widower, and he figured he was entitled to have his fling. What he had was a massive stroke, a series of them, the day he got the news about the fire. He was half paralyzed ever since, and he couldn't talk, or write. There was brain damage; we were never sure how bad. So," Tim said carefully, "when he had another stroke on December twenty-sixth, the general opinion was it was a blessing he never came out of it."

"What do you think?" I asked, not moving.

"I think," Tim said, "that somebody was to blame for what happened to him, *all* of it. And I don't mean Rowena, or her parents, or any 'accidents.' I've read everything that was written about the fire, including the insurance investigators' reports Gramps was sent. That's why I came here looking for a job, to try to find out if the fire was deliberate arson. And after all the rest of the Unicorn Farm curse garbage—"

"Don't."

"I'm sorry. I know it isn't funny. After the bacteria, and the deaths of the foals, I'm more sure than ever that the fire was set."

I said irrelevantly, "You never even told me your grandfather had died."

"I wanted to. But by that time I couldn't." Tim's mouth twisted. "Anyway, that's why I blew up at you on New Year's Eve. Because I knew from inside what you were going through, and how much harm those feelings could do if they were bottled up." He drew a deep breath. "Yes, I'm angry. Yes, I want revenge for my grandfather! But not from you! I never counted on falling in love with you. I've kept some things from you, but I've never lied to you about anything, not even my name, least of all my feelings. And either you believe that, or you don't."

I did believe him. Face your emotions, Tim had told me. I was facing them, and the bottom line was that trust was a gamble, love was a gamble, life was . . . just like horse racing. And I'd already, irrevocably, placed my bet.

I leaned forward, not reaching out with my hands, and I kissed him. And when the kiss ended, some while later, there was no need for further words on that subject.

"What did you mean," I asked hazily when I could think straight, "that the fire wasn't the cause of the curse, and revenge was not the reason?"

Tim looked at me. "Because somebody out for revenge would be trying to ruin Unicorn Farm permanently, and nobody is."

"But of course they are," I said stupidly. "The bacteria . . . the deaths . . ."

"You're seeing them the way you're supposed to see them," Tim said patiently. "Forget about the window dressing, and look at what's really happened. Both in the fire and since. Barns burned down. Rowena's parents died. Horses being boarded here died, and some of Unicorn Farm's own stock, not the most valuable. Even Bright Dancer and Shining Star weren't that. If somebody was trying to destroy Unicorn Farm permanently, the best way to do it would be to destroy its most valuable assets. What are they, Sarah? Think hard."

I frowned. "Now that you put it that way . . . Beauvais, I suppose. And Tapestry, and a couple of Beau's other stallion offspring. And my Starfire."

"Exactly," Tim said. "Hasn't it occurred to you that in the midst of all the accidents and sickness here, it's almost as if Beau and the other big-money horses are being very carefully protected?"

"What we have to do first," Tim said when I'd thought that over and seen his point, "is check into who stood to benefit by the fire, and how. And check people's alibis."

I shook my head. "What we have to do first is tell Rowena who you really are. And what we're suspecting." I stopped. "No. We won't tell her that till we check some people out."

I was thinking of Greg and Uncle Ned, and Tim knew it. "If we're on the right track, there's a very cool brain masterminding the whole 'curse' operation. And the whole thing revolves around money. For the life of me, I can't see how anybody benefited from the fire, except possibly by getting Gilbert Drake out of the way. But if you take things further—"

I sat up excitedly. "If you take things further, like two years further, and Rowena has debts she can't meet, and is losing money, what's apt to happen? If the only thing safe around here is the stallions?"

Tim struck his head. "Rowena will have to sell her livestock. Or syndicate it. She wouldn't make near as much money out of it as she could have before the killer bacteria struck, but once that story was lived down, whoever owned the syndication shares would make millions."

"And the two loudest voices urging her to sell out, or syndicate, belong to Greg Stahl and Dr. Drake. And Greg Stahl's known to pal around with gamblers." I took a deep breath. "So is, or was, Uncle Ned. I talked to Cyrus, like you told me to. Ned was disinherited because he gambled away one of his dad's prize stallions. And there's something else I haven't told you. The reason he stopped practicing medicine was that he made an error in an injection he gave once while he was drunk."

Tim whistled. "Did Cyrus tell you that?"

"No. Uncle Ned did. He said that's also what made him go on the wagon."

Tim looked at me. "Sarah, do you see? If there's some connection among all these things—Dr. Drake and gamblers, Dr. Drake and drinking, Dr. Drake and medical malpractice—" His eyes narrowed. "I wonder what happened to whoever received that botched injection. If the person died, and Dr. Drake's being blackmailed . . . Sarah, I think we're getting somewhere."

I found myself wishing that weren't true.

Tim invited himself to dinner, planning to break the news of his identity to Rowena afterward. But halfway through the meal Rowena put down her fork. "All right, you two. Spit it out. I can't eat any longer around your meaningful glances."

"Tim has something to tell you," I said bravely.

Rowena heard us through and then looked at us

with a Mona Lisa smile. "Do you really think I'm so haphazard about my choice of stablehands? Mr. Atkins was passing around Tim's high school graduation picture the last time I saw him. When Tim showed up here I recognized him right away." Our faces reddened, and she laughed. "If Tim didn't want to proclaim the relationship, that was all right with me. I respected him for trying to get the job without pull—even if I did suspect why he was doing it."

The next day was Sunday, which put a crimp in our plans for doing research, for insurance firms and other places we'd thought of contacting were closed. "And I have the reports Gramps was sent about the fire, and all the newspapers on it I could locate, in a bank safe deposit box downtown," Tim said. "I'll get them out first thing Monday."

First thing, of course, meant after stable chores were done, and that meant midmorning. By that time we were glad to leave the stable yard, for things there were sticky. Greg had come over, accompanied by Luke Hoyle. Greg had been adamant with Rowena: He was leaving Tapestry at the farm, and he was paying Luke to train him. K.T., who'd apparently been warned by Rowena, had rearranged her schedule and was not there, and Rowena took herself off downtown. That suited me down to the ground. While Helen Gallagher was having lunch, I helped myself to a lot of business office records and carried them to the manor house study.

Tim called the Jockey Club and the trainers' professional association, identifying himself as Simon Atkins's grandson and inquiring into the credentials of Luke Hoyle. They checked out: impeccable. I checked Unicorn Farm's medical insurance program records and found that Uncle Ned, as the farm's consulting geneticist, was covered; checked the files and found the name and number of the "drying-out tank" he had referred to. With my hand on the telephone buttons, I paused.

"I feel sneaky, doing this."

"You have the most right; you're family." And the most duty, I thought as Tim went on. "Will it make you feel any different to know that K.T.'s lost two of her regular jobs because of the rumor about her mishandling the injection?"

I pushed buttons. I told the starchy voice that answered that I was the executive secretary of Unicorn Farm and was verifying back records for tax purposes.

Dr. Ned Drake had been incarcerated, very much under observation, for one month before and three months following the fire.

I went back further into Unicorn Farm's records, hoping to find information about the botched injection that had caused him to give up practicing medicine. I even, uneasily, went through the files in the locked bottom drawer of Rowena's desk, the drawer she'd told me contained her will and other personal and family papers.

"I want you to know where they are, and have this key, just in case you need access and I'm—not available," she had said to me a few days after Christmas. I knew she'd meant in case any "accident" happened to her. I considered preventing such an event important enough to justify my actions. The drawer contained a lot of things about Uncle Ned, some of them embarrassing, like a copy of the letter his father had sent disinheriting him. It had given dates and names. But there was nothing remotely similar pertaining to Uncle Ned's monumental, and disastrous, drunken error. Only a few postcards from him to Rowena, with assorted postmarks ... New York, Florida, Las Vegas. Then—I started. A receipt for his first stay at the sanatorium, four years ago! And a copy of a Las Vegas police report, detailing Uncle Ned's arrest for driving while intoxicated. It was for a date two days before his transfer to the sanatorium.

"Call the Las Vegas police," Tim said. And when I made no move, he did it for me, pretending to be my brother. Yes, the records of the arrest were still available. Sentence had been suspended contingent on Dr. Drake's leaving Nevada and entering a sanatorium. No, there was no record of malpractice, or involvement in any accident. (I was being very cautious, not mentioning the drug-related death.) Nothing of the sort had happened during the six weeks Dr. Drake had been in the city, although he had built up a considerable record as a belligerent alcoholic.

I called the American Medical Association. They had a clean record on Dr. Edward Drake—no charges ever registered against him.

I even, taking a deep breath, called Rowena's insurance firms. There had never been a claim registered against Dr. Drake. "We would know, because we covered him for malpractice when he was still a practicing physician. Why did he stop? We understood for personal reasons." From the tone in the agent's voice, I interpreted that to mean his drinking problem.

When I hung up, my heart was heavy. "There's no record that he ever harmed anybody with the wrong drug. Maybe he made the whole story up to excuse his refusing to help with the horses."

"Or else he paid off the guy's family, so a claim would not be filed. Which would go a long way to explain his destitution!" Tim looked at me. "You've investigated Rowena's private papers. Don't you think it's time you investigated the doctor's too?"

"I couldn't! Think of what would happen if he caught me!"

"Think of what could happen if you don't," Tim said flatly. "Where is the doctor, anyway?"

"Out. He's been out most of the time the past three days." I frowned. "That's unusual, come to think of it. He's kept very close to home ever since he got back from that last trip."

Tim reached for the phone and called a number. "Chuck? It's me. Look, is the doctor there? . . . No, don't call him! Just keep him there! Take his keys away from him if you can manage to. I'll come collect him in half an hour or so.

"I'm sorry, Sarah," he said, putting down the phone. "I didn't want to dump anything more on you and Rowena until I had to. He's off the wagon again. He's passing out regularly down at the tavern where the stable crew hangs out. So regularly he's hired me to get him home if the bartender phones me."

"You should have told us."

"I figured he could do less harm passed out than running around as a suspect," Tim pointed out logically. "At least we know he can't walk in on us now. Come on."

We searched his room, finding nothing worse than a pile of filthy laundry and some mildly dirty books. Then we went up to the third floor.

It was the first time I'd crossed the threshold of the doctor's sanctum, and I didn't know what to expect. Certainly nothing remotely like it was, which was a cross between a Victorian opium den and Sherlock Holmes's Baker Street study. Dingy, nicotine-stained wallpaper covered the sloping walls. Dark wood made bookcases in them, and framed bare windows. Everywhere, everywhere there were books and papers ... on the shelves, on the big battered desk and the sway-seated leather sofa, on the floor, on tables. A deer's head leered at me from above the fireplace, and stuffed owls perched on the mantel. A skull sat on a stained table next to a chemistry set, a microscope, and a Bunsen burner. Tim started for that, then stopped.

"We'd better be methodical. Divide the room into sections and do one at a time."

"I'll start at this end," I said, heading for the desk. He went to the fireplace and we started, each covering one square yard at a time, restoring everything we touched to its prior disorder.

We expected to meet in the center, but we didn't get that far. I had with difficulty done the desk and was going through the lower shelves of the nearest built-in bookcase, when my fingers found a knothole in the back wall. I pulled books off the shelves and explored the knothole carefully.

One whole plank of wood fell out of the back wall. Inside were papers that I unfolded with suddenly clumsy fingers. The first was the original of the scathing letter from his father. The second one—

I scanned it swiftly, then again; then the other papers inside. Then I let out a cry.

"Tim! You were right! He *did* pay off for that botched injection privately! Only it wasn't just a botched injection! There's a copy of a death certificate here—for somebody named Arthur Sims."

"What did he die of?" Tim asked over his shoulder.

I scanned the paper. Then I gasped. "A *car accident*. That's what the certificate says. Arthur Sims was killed in a car crash outside Las Vegas." I fumbled through the other papers hurriedly. "Here's an obituary—Sims ran his car off the road, driving while intoxicated. The whole thing went up in flames."

"How did they know he was drunk, then?" Tim muttered. .

"There were witnesses—he was seen behaving drunkenly in a casino, fifteen minutes earlier. He was seen driving all over the road, heading for that curve ... *Tim*! The man died in a crash, so why did Uncle Ned give a certified check for two hundred fifty thousand dollars to a Melva Sims two days later?"

But I knew the answer. Death benefits—for a death whose true cause had been hushed up. Uncle Ned had paid, to avoid a malpractice suit, loss of his medical license, a manslaughter charge, or worse. He was still paying. "Tim, there's an IOU here for over a million dollars, payable on demand from Uncle Ned to some company called Sims and Alberti! And there's a letter to Melva Sims from a James Alberti—"

I broke off before I could tell Tim that the letter confirmed what I'd already realized about a coverup, for Tim was interrupting me, in a tight, even voice I'd never heard him use.

"Sarah, go down to the kitchen and get some of those Ziploc plastic bags. And some pill bottles. Dump out the contents, and sterilize them well, and bring them here. Just maybe I've found the secret of the killer bacteria."

He was holding, gingerly and with Kleenex, a half-filled hypodermic and an assortment of vials.

I have never wanted to be an actress, but for the next several days I lived an act. Both Tim and I did. We agreed it would be cruel to tell Rowena what we now knew, and suspected, about Dr. Drake. Not without proof. Even if he had been guilty of manslaughter, he'd given up the practice of medicine, after all. We couldn't prove he was or was not responsible for the happenings at Unicorn Farm. In the back of our minds was the awareness that we had not yet cleared or indicted Greg Stahl, either. Either way, Rowena would be deeply hurt.

What we did do that Monday afternoon was to put the chemicals Tim had found in carefully sterilized bottles and Ziploc bags. Then Tim took off to find Dr. Lang. We agreed that Tim would, after swearing the professor to secrecy, tell him the whole story (except for the Las Vegas incident) and ask him to get the specimens analyzed by the appropriate authorities. Tim would then go to his bank, get the items he'd personally been collecting as evidence out of his safe deposit box, and bring them and Uncle Ned back to Unicorn Farm.

I, meanwhile, took Greg up on his invitation to visit Haseley Hall anytime I wanted. I got him talking about his past as I followed him around. I was so successful that Greg ended sitting down with me in his posh study and telling me the story of his life—complete with scrapbooks, photograph albums, and awards and clippings in four languages. Greg's life since his university graduation was so well-documented it was hard to believe it could have any secret moments.

He was having such a good time telling me the story that he telephoned Rowena and invited her to join us there for dinner, and succeeded in completely charming her out of her displeasure on the subject of Luke Hoyle. He even, almost, made me forget my eagerness to hear from Tim about his meeting with Dr. Lang. You're a dangerous man, Gregory Stahl, I thought to myself; brains, and a cool head, and power, and charm enough to have kissed an Alpine Blarney Stone. And animal magnetism. Definitely, animal magnetism.

We reached home very late to find the telephone ringing. "Where have you been?" Tim demanded.

"Over at Haseley Hall for dinner. There was no way I could get away. How did you make out?"

"Okay," Tim said guardedly. "Tell Rowena Dr. Drake's decided to sign himself into that fancy rest home over in Louisville for a week or so."

"How did you pull that off?"

"I packed his bag for him and took him over."

That would keep the doctor under wraps at least for a time. And give us a chance to check on the Simses and James Alberti, whose names were on that IOU—and to get the analyses back on those specimens. "How did things go otherwise?" I asked, equally cagy.

"Great. I'd hoped to take you out to talk awhile, but it's so late we'll have to wait for tomorrow."

We had to wait, in fact, until we were eating a fast food lunch under our favorite tree on campus. There could be both privacy and safety in public places, and there was scant chance of the wrong people overhearing here.

"How did you really get Uncle Ned to go?" I asked abruptly. "You didn't say anything to make him suspect?"

Tim shook his head. "I reminded him that he'd hired me to drive for him, and told him that if he cared enough about his health to do that, he ought to listen to me now and check himself in somewhere."

"Okay. And how did Dr. Lang react when you saw him?"

"Great. Thank God for the scientific mind! He's having the specimens analyzed as if they're from the university lab, but he warned me that if what we suspect shows up in them, he'll have to tell the whole truth to the authorities."

I nodded. "We'll all have to. But till then ..." I left the phrase unfinished.

A few days went by. April unfolded in a burst of flowering glory. Young foals cavorted with their mothers in the paddocks. Tim and I waited for news from Dr. Lang. No other crises occurred.

I went to a bank in Lexington, rented a safe deposit box, and put in it the papers I'd found in Uncle Ned's wall hiding place. Greg decided to enter Tapestry in the Blue Grass Stakes, and had Luke train him daily. K.T. could not avoid being at Unicorn Farm when he was there, now, but they ignored each other's existence as stallions in neighboring paddocks did. Greg also decided that Rowena must go with him to the Lexington Ball at Spendthrift Farm, and in a munificent gesture bought tickets for Tim and me as well. He knew now about Tim's true identity, because Rowena told him. The other stablehands accepted it matter-of-factly. Tim was already one of them. Cy, I suspected, had long since guessed Tim's secret.

Rowena decided that we might as well buy ball gowns for the Lexington Ball, and we drove over to Louisville on Saturday. We stayed overnight at a hotel, and on Sunday morning visited Churchill Downs, where the Derby would be held in four more weeks. She told me stories about her jockey days. We met no one that we knew. It was a fun, carefree escape. Late on Sunday afternoon we returned to Unicorn Farm and found it as I'd remembered it, slumbering in golden peace.

No visitors had been over, the guard at the gate reported. We drove up the avenue of trees and around to the stable yard, and everything was gilded with a pre-sunset glow. Shadow rolled on his back, trying to attract the attention of a bored cat. Beau was racing and braking like a yearling in his paddock. Nothing else stirred, except for Cyrus ambling out of the stallion barn chewing on a blade of grass.

"Miss D, I wish you'd come and take a look at Tapestry. He isn't acting himself. Hasn't been since Hoyle brung him back from training yesterday. He's kind of off his feed, so I kept him in his stall till you come back."

Not the bacteria . . . the same thought leaped

into both our minds; I could see it in Rowena's frightened eyes. Then Cyrus shook his head.

"He's not sick. Just not himself. Acts a little lame, like he did before. I thought maybe he got a burr in his hoof or something, but he won't let me near him."

"I'll come," Rowena said promptly. I began to follow, but Cy stopped me.

"Tim Payne's waiting up at the house for you. Been on pins and needles for the past hour."

I started for the back door, where I could see Tim sitting with barely contained patience. "Give me some peppermints," I heard Rowena say to Cyrus. "Tapestry loves them now as much as Beau does." I kept on going.

I had just reached the bottom step, and Tim was rising, holding out an envelope, when we heard the first scream.

Without thought, purely on instinct, we turned and started running. Tim had longer legs and he outdistanced me, and I pelted after. And all the time, from the stallion barn, the shrieks went on: Rowena's, screaming for help, screaming horse commands. Cyrus's, high-pitched—yelling for Tim; turning into a screech of pain; cut off abruptly. The shriek of an enraged stallion. From the far paddock, Beau, screaming in sympathy.

I burst into the barn to an appalling sight. Tapestry's wrought-iron gate was shut and latched. Beyond it in his stall the stallion reared in fury, flailing with his hooves. Rowena was between him and Cyrus, who was crumpled like a broken puppet against a bale of hay. Blood trickled from his nose and mouth, and his eyes were closed. Rowena was trying to hold Tapestry off with a pitchfork she'd snatched

off a wall hook. It had already drawn blood on him,
but he paid no heed.

Tim had seized a whip and was trying to undo
the latch.

"No!" I screamed. "No, you could be killed!"

"Don't let him loose!" Rowena shouted. "Phone
for help."

She was tiring rapidly. Tim vaulted over the
gate, whip in his teeth, as I dove for the phone. I
shouted into the intercom for the security guards
and then, as if on instinct, phoned Haseley Hall.

Behind me, Tim's whip snapped, and the horse
keened in panic. Rowena screamed once, sharply.
Then, simultaneously and with almost unbelievable
speed, the security guards and Greg arrived on the
scene. Greg was on Maximilian, and he rode right
into the barn. He swung down, and as Max edged
away from Tapestry, Greg pushed the guards aside.

I gazed, horror-stricken, past him into the stall.

Tim, his back to the gate, was keeping Tapestry
off with the whip. Tapestry, lunging back, had Rowena pinned down on the hay. Her leg was bent
under her at a crazy angle, and as we watched,
Tapestry's hooves came down hard upon it.

"You have a gun. Use it," Greg snapped to the
nearest security guard.

Rowena cried out in protest. The guard seemed
frozen. With one swift gesture Greg snatched the
weapon from its holster, checked it for bullets, and
took deliberate aim at the stallion's head.

There was an explosion, and spurting blood, and
the animal fell directly on Rowena.

At that, everyone was galvanized. Tim jerked the
inside latch open. Greg sprang to Rowena. The guards
pulled Tapestry's body from her with difficulty. I

was on the telephone, calling the police to send an ambulance. Tim knelt by Cyrus.

Rowena was conscious, barely, holding tightly to Greg's hand. I knew from Tim's face that the old groom was dead.

The police arrived, with sirens screaming, and confirmed it. The ambulance attendants lifted Rowena carefully onto a stretcher and Cy, with less care, onto another. Greg and Tim and I followed the ambulance in Rowena's car, after Greg had had curt words with the security guards and they'd discovered the barn's TV cameras had been turned off. Carelessness? Deliberate malice?

No one, I kept telling myself, not even Uncle Ned, could have caused Tapestry to attack Rowena. It still seemed impossible it could have happened.

But it was real. Rowena's compound fracture of the leg was real. So were the deaths of Tapestry and Cyrus.

I was with Rowena at the hospital when she came back, barely conscious, from having her leg set, and the first thing she asked me was about Cyrus. I told her, gently. Rowena squeezed my hand. "See to him, Sarah ..."

"I will. I promise."

"He has a grandson out west, somewhere. Only relative. It will be in the files."

"I know. I'll find it. Rowena, I'll take care of everything. Don't think about any of it now—just rest." The emergency room doctor had already told us she was fighting against sedation.

"Sarah, don't stay here. Have Tim take you home. You can stay at Haseley Hall."

"No, I can't," I said firmly. "I can stay in my own bedroom. And I'll ask Tim to stay, too. In the guest room, I mean."

I was relieved when, as I'd hoped, Rowena chuckled.

"You may as well all go home," the doctor said. "She'll be fine now, but she won't make much sense till morning." Greg refused to leave, though he wasn't allowed to stay in her room because he was not related. We left him in the visitors' lounge, dictating a stream of orders into the telephone. One of them was the firing of Luke Hoyle.

Tim drove us home. "Want to stop for something to eat?" he asked.

I realized with a start that it was now well after nine P.M. "We can fix something at home. There's too much to do." Locating Cyrus's grandson and telling him, I thought. Calling a funeral home. Deciding what to tell the newspapers for an obituary. All the details that had descended on me in the hours after Mother's death flashed back vividly, and I shuddered. Tim put his arm around me, and drove the rest of the way one-handed.

The gates of Unicorn Farm were bolted. Tim leaned on the horn, and soon a security guard drove down the drive to let us in. "Since those cameras in the barn were monkeyed with, we figured we'd better take no chances with the intercom and the electronic controls out here," he commented.

"They were tampered with, then?"

"Had to be," he said briefly. "I checked the cameras myself this morning."

"You're doing double shift today?" Tim asked, eyes narrowing.

"Security chief called four of us back on duty." The guard turned to me, his manner showing clearly that in Rowena's absence I had become the boss. "We need extra coverage till we sort out what's been going on. The police sergeant wanted you to call him as soon as you got back."

I nodded. Tim drove up the drive, now lit by every floodlight the farm possessed. "Park at the front door," I said. "That's closest to the road in case—in case we have to go anywhere in a hurry." Despite the orthopedist's reassurances, I was deeply worried about Rowena.

"Think positive," Tim said gently. He kissed me, then got out and came round to open my door. He held out both hands to me, and I started.

"What is it?" he said quickly.

"When you held out your hands ... I'm trying to remember. *Tim!* When you did that earlier, when you were waiting for me on the back steps before everything happened, didn't you have an envelope in your hands?"

Tim stared at me, the color draining from his face. "Good God," he said slowly. "The test results ... Sarah, there *were* bacteria spores in those samples."

I jumped out of the car and we both started running. Around to the back—there was nothing lying on the steps or the back path. There was no brown envelope lying anywhere in the stable yard. There was none in the kitchen, where we illogically looked as soon as I had fumbled for the back door key.

I leaped for the telephone and buzzed frantically for the security chief. "We've set up a temporary operations center in the business office," he said. I'd forgotten he'd been provided with keys for all the buildings. "A brown envelope? Yes, one of my men found it. I'll send it over."

He brought it personally. "How is Miss Drake? Miss Burton, I'd like a conference with you at your earliest convenience."

"At nine in the morning. Continue the extra manpower in the meantime." My mind was on the lab

SHADOW OF A UNICORN

report, and I saw with relief that the envelope was sealed.

"I went ahead and read it. And when you weren't here, I put it into another envelope from the business office and sealed it up." Tim inspected that carefully. "It's the same one. I'd been handling newspapers, and my fingers were inky. There are still my fingerprints along the seal."

I sat down at the kitchen table and started to read as Tim began moving quietly around assembling one of his impromptu pastas. Several of the samples we'd taken from the upstairs study had been innocuous. Three had contained live bacteria—one a type known to cause severe inflammation; the other two the "mystery killer" strain.

"Dear God," I whispered.

"The Type A bacteria would explain the limp Tapestry had last fall," Tim said, watching me as he chopped onions. "The other definitely accounts for the stallion deaths this year. Whether the earlier deaths were caused by inoculation, or whether these cultures were made from specimens taken from the first dead horse, we don't know yet."

"This will just about kill Rowena."

"We don't know for sure what Dr. Drake's part in all this is. Keep reading."

The report went on with an analysis of the muscle relaxant K.T. had administered. It was triple the strength specified on the bottle's label. I grasped at straws. "Luke picked this up at the pharmacy."

"I must admit he's my favorite candidate," Tim confessed. "But the bottle was sealed when he handed it to Dr. Drake. We all watched Doc open it and measure the dose, and watched K.T. give the injection. There was no chance for hanky-panky, as he calls it, then. So we still don't know when and how the stuff was doctored. Unless you suspect the pharmacist!"

"He's about the only person I don't suspect," I said grimly. "Everybody else could have a motive we don't know about. Even Dr. Voelkner. Even Greg."

"Even me."

I shook my head. "Not you. You lost from the fire. You didn't gain from it. And you won't gain anything if Unicorn Farm goes down the drain with the stallions unharmed."

I remembered then that one of those very valuable stallions now was gone.

"Doesn't it strike you as funny," Tim said, "that Stahl shot Tapestry so fast? And gave orders to get rid of the carcass so fast? He ordered it to be cremated at once, *all* of it," he added as I stared. "What did he pay Rowena for him, anyway? About a million?"

"It shows how rich he is. And how much he loves Rowena. He didn't risk her life one extra second."

"Stahl loves money too. And horses. I'm not implying that he doesn't love her. But he didn't even *try* to calm the horse first, and he's good at that."

I stood up abruptly. "I don't want to hear any more. Not right now! I'm so confused I—isn't that mess you're cooking ready yet? I have to start calling around about poor old Cyrus."

"You have to call the police," Tim said.

"Not yet. I need to think first. If we could tie Luke in with those people Uncle Ned owes money to ... Maybe Uncle Ned *wasn't* involved in the Unicorn curse. Maybe he caught on to it, and took these samples as evidence so *he* could try a little blackmail.... I have to let him know about Rowena."

"Let him sleep till morning. It's practically the middle of the night now," Tim said firmly. He dished me a plate of spaghetti that I ate dutifully. After that I put the specimens and accompanying report in the study safe. Tim walked me out to the business office and I looked up the name and address of Cyrus's grandson.

Tim looked at it over my shoulder, and whistled. "Do you get the feeling everything's turning into a corny film script?" The grandson lived in Las Vegas.

"The police can check that angle out later. Whether he's tied in some way or not, he has to be called," I said, and did so. It wasn't till around two-thirty A.M. that I reached him. The grandson turned out to be a musician at a Vegas hotel. He said he couldn't fly east for another two days, and would I please make arrangements for a funeral. Something Cyrus would like; not too expensive. "Unicorn Farm will take care of the cost," I said coldly.

Tim and I never got to sleep all night. At five in the morning, knowing the Haseley Hall stud would already be operational, I called and asked for Greg. He had not been home all night. Tapestry? According to Mr. Stahl's orders, the stallion's body had been loaded into a van and driven to the crematorium most of the breeders used. I was given the phone number. There was no answer at it until nine A.M., and by then the body had already been reduced to ashes.

Tim was right; it had happened awfully fast. What was I suspecting, anyway, I wondered. The bacteria wouldn't have made Tapestry attack Cy or Rowena. But some other drug?

I called Dr. Voelkner and told him what had happened. I called the hospital. Rowena was resting comfortably. Greg was still there and had insisted on Rowena's being transferred to a luxury room with round-the-clock special nurses, all of which were to be billed to Haseley Hall. "Mr. Stahl particularly didn't want you waked to give permission, Miss Burton. Since he and Miss Drake are in a business partnership, and Haseley Hall's insurance will be covering the accident, we were sure it was in order." It was clear that Greg had charmed the hospital staff. And had stretched the truth.

And meanwhile poor Cyrus was lying in the hospital morgue, unclaimed. I had my phone call transferred there. The autopsy had been completed— death by asphyxiation as result of chest crushed by horse—and the police had authorized the body's release. I said it would be called for. I looked in the study files, found the name of the funeral director that had handled Uncle Gil's and Aunt Roberta's funeral, and called him. "We'll send a hearse for the remains at once. The same funeral arrangements that Miss Drake made for her parents? Yes, of course. If you'd come down and pick out a casket sometime this morning, we'll take care of everything else. We'll take care of death notices and the obituary. Cyrus was a famous local character, you know. We were all shocked when we read about the accident in the morning paper."

That last sent us rushing to the front door as soon as I'd hung up. The paper, brought up from the gate by the security guard, was on the doorstep, neatly folded. "Curse Strikes Unicorn Farm Again" was a front-page story.

"Uncle Ned! I have to reach him before he sees this!" I cried.

"Why?" Tim asked flatly.

"No matter what else he might have done, he would never have put Rowena's life in danger. I *know* that, Tim. I have to let him know she's okay." As I said it, I realized that I knew something else about Dr. Drake. He would never, no matter how resentful about his disinheritance, have deliberately caused his brother's death. *That meant that, even if Uncle Ned had doped the horses, someone else had masterminded everything, starting with the fire.* All this flashed through my mind as I ran for the phone.

I got the sanatorium. They were sorry. Dr. Drake was not available. He had checked out two hours ago. Had he seen the morning paper? Why yes, that was sent in on all the breakfast trays.

"Call the police," Tim said promptly.

"No! Not till I've talked with him. We'll just sit tight until he gets here."

The police didn't let me wait. They came to me. I answered all their questions, volunteering nothing, saying nothing about the lab reports or specimens. Tim, looking unhappy, did the same. "I'll give you another three hours," he said to me when the police were gone, "then *I'll* tell them. I arranged for those tests to be done, remember."

"Uncle Ned will be here any minute!"

But he wasn't. "He could have gone to the hospital," Tim said, and called there. Several people had called or come, but Rowena was not being allowed visitors yet, and all had been turned away. Dr. Drake had not been among them.

"If he does know who's behind the curse, he

could be hiding. Or out looking for them." I paced with my hands clenched, thinking hard. "He took off this winter, right when everything here hit rock bottom. Strange men who wouldn't leave their names kept phoning for him, and they sounded downright nasty. When he did come back, he kept such a low profile."

"Which wasn't like him," Tim agreed. "What are you thinking?"

"I'm not sure, but I'm getting scared." I whirled around. "Tim, we've got to find him. Before anything else happens. It can't be another coincidence, his signing out of the hospital and disappearing right after he read the paper!"

Tim was already reaching for the phone. He called the usual tavern, sounding casual. Dr. Drake had not been seen. No, no one else had been asking for him. Tim hung up and rose.

"I'll take the van and go out looking. I know his usual haunts. Sarah, stay here. If anything, *anything* happens, for heaven's sake, phone the police!"

I did phone the police soon after he left, but it was to ask about the reliability of the security force that we employed. It had suddenly dawned on me that they, like Luke Hoyle, had come to Unicorn Farm at Greg Stahl's recommendation. The police sergeant laughed. "Don't you worry about them, Miss Burton. They're the best you can get, and they're all ex-policemen. You don't go getting yourself worked up about that newspaper nonsense, hear?"

It was clear that the police had decided yesterday's catastrophe was accidental.

The back doorbell rang, and it was Mr. Beech. "I didn't want to bother you earlier, figured you'd have buzzed me if you needed to. I just want to tell you the day's work's been done. The horses are back out in the paddocks, and the stallion barn's been cleaned so well you'd never know what happened." His formal manner softened. "Everybody feels bad. The boys chipped in to send Miss D flowers, and they want to know about the arrangements for Cy so they can pay respects."

I provided the information, and he nodded.

"Sounds what Cy would have liked. I'll meet the grandson's plane tomorrow. Cy worked directly under me." Mr. Beech started to go, then paused. "I still can't understand what made Tapestry turn maverick. Temperamental, yes, but not mean. Must have been the result of Hoyle's training. I phoned Haseley Hall," he added grimly, "to give that conceited goon a piece of my mind. But nobody'd seen hide nor hair of him since Friday."

After Tom Beech left, the house seemed extra empty. The clock in the hall ticked inexorably. It was three in the afternoon, and I still hadn't eaten lunch, let alone breakfast. I foraged in the refrigerator and found bread and cheese, and when I was just finishing it, the telephone rang.

I jumped for it, expecting to hear Tim's voice. I didn't.

"Sarah? Thank the good Lord. How is Rowena?"

It was Uncle Ned.

"**W**here are you?" I shouted.

"Shut up and listen!" Uncle Ned snapped with his customary asperity. And with something else, something I didn't have time to interpret, for he rushed on. "How bad is Rowena? The way that damn rumor sheet sounded, I didn't know what—"

"She'll be all right," I interrupted. "Where are you? Tim's out looking for you."

"I don't intend to be found if I can help it," Uncle Ned said testily. "Is it true about Cyrus? And that the horse attacked them?"

"Yes. Greg shot him." I wet my lips. "Uncle Ned, get in a taxi and come back here. Everything's going to be all right now."

"First I'm going to make sure of that." His voice hardened. "As soon as I read that thing, I knew I had to. It's my fault, the whole damn thing's my fault—"

"*Uncle Ned!* I know about the IOUs. I know about the injections—"

"Thank God." He sounded as if he meant it. "There won't be any more of it, Sarah. Tell Rowena that." His voice dropped. "I don't know how much time I have, so just listen. I am going to take care of everything. As soon as I've checked the final forty." What was that supposed to mean, I wondered blankly—forty-proof liquor in a drink? Had he fallen off the wagon *again?*

Joltingly, he gave a harsh laugh. "Tell Stahl not to give up hope. He still may win the Derby. And if I'm not home by dark, call the police."

The phone went dead.

I did what I should have done hours ago. I called the police right then and told them about everything from finding the specimens in Uncle Ned's attic to his latest phone call.

They pumped me over the phone, and in the background I heard another voice putting out an all points bulletin for Dr. Edward Drake. Description? I provided it swiftly. "I really don't think he's dangerous to anybody! He's terribly upset about his niece."

"We'll find that out as soon as we talk to him. If he calls again, Miss Burton, tell him to turn himself in. It will be in his own best interest and for his own protection." The officer hung up, leaving me wondering if Uncle Ned could have been contemplating suicide.

Ten minutes later the police arrived to pick up the lab reports and specimens and to turn me inside out with questions. Then, with my permission, they searched Uncle Ned's bedroom and his study. When they looked at the IOUs, I knew at once that they recognized the names Alberti and Sims.

When I asked, I received a lecture rather than an answer. "You know thoroughbred breeding's a big-time industry, don't you, Miss Burton? You and your cousin might have saved some lives if you'd brought us your suspicions earlier."

Both human and animal ones, I thought heavily, when they were gone. Dusk was falling outside the window, and I remembered what Uncle Ned had said about waiting until dark. Did he think something was waiting out there for him? Or was he actually, like an elderly Don Quixote, going out to do battle with the "curse" of Unicorn Farm?

I was getting light-headed. I wished Tim would return. Who knew where he might be looking for Uncle Ned, I thought. Who knew what anyone else would do, really? Or could do. I'd lived and done a lot I'd never thought I could have. I'd written Uncle Ned off as a harmless bumbler when I'd first known him, but now . . . I'd thought, we'd all thought, that Tapestry could never deliberately harm anyone.

Cyrus had said Tapestry wasn't acting himself.

He'd been off his feed.

Tom Beech said he couldn't understand what made Tapestry change so. That it must have been the result of Luke Hoyle's training.

And he loved peppermints, but Rowena's trying to give him some had driven him wild. It was as if he'd turned into a different horse.

Suppose it hadn't been Tapestry, but a look-alike that responded violently to peppermint, that had killed Cyrus and almost killed Rowena? And then been disposed of, before substitution could become known?

That last would mean Greg had been a part of the deception, but I rushed past that as illumination after illumination flooded through me. The horse attack was what had been the final straw for Uncle Ned, the thing that had caused him to rebel against his blackmailers—I was sure they were blackmailers now.

Uncle Ned had said to call the police if he weren't back by dark. If Uncle Ned were killed, the men who held his IOU could take his Unicorn Farm, Inc., stock in settlement of his debt to them. If *Rowena* had been killed, her shares would have gone to Uncle Ned and me. And how much would my life be worth, I thought, shivering. Or maybe I'd be safe. If I owned Unicorn Farm, I'd have to syndicate the stallions; I couldn't afford to keep the place going otherwise. Once that happened, the shares the gamblers owned would be worth millions.

A million dollars had gone up in the smoke of the gun that killed Tapestry. But maybe not. Maybe Tapestry was still alive somewhere. *That* would prove the frame-up.

Uncle Ned had said he was going to put a stop to everything, once he had checked the final forty. *Final forty.* Farmers talked about their fields in terms of forties, and Uncle Ned had grown up on this farm. Could he have been referring to the back paddocks, way back by the woodland that separated Unicorn Farm from Haseley Hall? The paddocks had been unused, I knew, since the fire that had decimated the farm's breeding stock. But Greg and Rowena often galloped through there.

I wasn't light-headed anymore. Or if I was, the lightness had crystallized into steely purpose. I wished to heaven Tim were here, but he wasn't, and dusk was thickening by the minute. I snatched a pen and piece of paper, and considered. Who knew who might find my note, and who knew who could be trusted? I scrawled hastily, "See you where we talked that Saturday," and left it prominently on the kitchen table.

Then I pulled on a sweater, grabbed a flashlight, and hurried out back. The fastest way, and quietest, to get around the horse farms was on horseback, so I saddled Jeeter. Carefully, my eyes traveling from left to right, I rode along past the apple orchards. Past Tapestry's empty paddock. Past Beauvais's, behind it. He was, as usual, in the far back reaches. But he recognized me, and he whinnied.

Was I going crazy, or was there an answering whinny from beyond? I dug my heels into Jeeter and galloped on. Poor Jeeter was tiring. I slowed and, scanning the first empty paddock, peered into the wooded area beyond. I didn't want to risk the flashlight.

Something moved.

I slid down from Jeeter's back and looped his reins around a fence rail. Then, my heart beginning to pound, I whinnied.

It sounded, deliberately, like Beauvais. Somebody listening could think it was Beauvais again.

Somebody—something—did think so. An answering whinny came from beneath the trees. A shape emerged, prancing. Came toward me; stopped.

Sometime during last night's sleeplessness, I'd changed into jeans. I thrust my hand into their pocket now and pulled out a roll of peppermints. Their pungency carried on the April breeze, and Tapestry did a little dance.

"I thought you'd show yourself for these," I murmured softly.

A flashlight beam shot out of the darkness, blinding me. "You'd have been better off if he hadn't, Miss Burton."

I couldn't see him, but I knew from the taunt and the tone that it was Luke Hoyle. Then the beam moved slightly, and I could see his shape, and the gleam of a gun barrel. The gun gestured.

"Over by the fence, Miss Burton. Nice and easy."

"You can't get the horse to do your killing for you this time," I said with spirit. "Or do you intend to shoot me by accident while you're killing the horse to save me?"

"Not a chance," Luke said silkily. "This beast's worth too much. I think an accident will take care of it. Or suicide. A teenager, distraught over her mother's death, goes over the edge after weird things start happening here?"

"I'll cause an accident, you swine," somebody else said sardonically.

Uncle Ned. He, too, had a gun—Lord only knew where he'd gotten it—and it was pointing directly at Luke Hoyle's back. He moved purposefully toward the trainer. "Alberti sent you here, didn't he?" he asked.

Luke turned slightly, managing a sneer. "I don't know what you're talking about."

"Yes, you do," Uncle Ned said calmly. "Jim Alberti, my old pal from college days. Who led me astray, with my enthusiastic cooperation. Who was so helpful when I accidentally killed his buddy, Arthur Sims. It took me a while to realize Jim was really happy about that. He saw a way to move in on Unicorn Farm—buying it, buying syndicate shares. Only he didn't know I had no authority here—not even after my brother died. Not till Rowena, the dear fool, gave me a share."

Uncle Ned chuckled, sending a shiver up my spine. "Jim didn't realize that at my age, life and reputation can suddenly seem less important than family does."

His finger tightened on the trigger. Luke started to move, then froze.

"*Move*, Sarah!" Uncle Ned snapped at me. "Go get the security guards."

I eased myself away as Luke, at Uncle Ned's command, threw down his gun. Only then, in a lightning flash, as the doctor tried to circle around him, Luke spun. There was a brief struggle and an old man's cry. And then, just as I was diving for Luke's dropped weapon, Uncle Ned's gun was in Luke's hands.

It was pointing directly at me.

"You old fool," Luke said contemptuously for Uncle Ned's benefit. His eyes, and the gun barrel, were straight on me.

Everything seemed to go into slow motion then. He has to shoot me first, I was thinking. If he turned to aim at Uncle Ned, I could get his own gun, and he knows it. Only maybe he isn't absolutely sure what Uncle Ned will do. I gathered my muscles together, poised for that single moment when Luke's concentration might waver.

In a moment outside of time, Uncle Ned threw himself between Luke's gun and me.

The gun blazed, and as Uncle Ned fell, I moved. Out of the flashlight's beam, into the almost total darkness. I fell to the ground and went absolutely silent.

Uncle Ned made no sound.

Luke swept up the other gun and swung himself up onto Tapestry's back. He wasn't going to waste time on me. He was getting out of there before he could be stopped—heading, probably, toward where he'd ditched a car.

He was headed, not toward Unicorn Farm and its guards, but toward Haseley Hall.

I had to stop him, and there was only one way that I even stood a chance. As soon as I was sure he could no longer hear me, I scrambled to my feet and started running. Not toward Jeeter. Jeeter wasn't a racehorse, and he was tired. I ran toward Beauvais, and I whinnied. And when I dared, I called. Wildly.

Beauvais came. His huge blackness was silhouetted against a moonlit sky as he cleared the paddock fences exactly as he'd cleared the obstacles in the steeplechase. He braked beside me, standing quietly, and I took hold of his mane and pulled myself up onto his back. Then I twisted my fingers into that mane, leaned against his neck, and whispered.

"Go, Beau! Go to Haseley Hall!"

Beau went. I had all I could do to just hang on. But Beau, with just the same sixth sense he'd always shown for Rowena, went like a silent wind. Not through the open passageways. Through the woods, and over brooks and fences, just as he had done with Rowena when they practiced for the steeplechase.

It was the one way we could get to Haseley Hall without being seen. And we could do it faster than Luke could get off the Haseley Hall grounds by car.

We tore into the drive of Haseley Hall and came to a stop beside the black Mercedes Greg had just driven home.

I fell off Beauvais's back into Greg Stahl's arms, and after that things started seeming like I was in a time warp. How many times now, I wondered hysterically, had I dealt with life and death?

I gasped out my story, and Greg's security staff called the police and fanned out in search of Luke. Greg and I went hurtling back in the Mercedes toward the paddock.

Uncle Ned was dead. I'd known he was. I would never forget that he died protecting me.

The police collected Tim in their sweep, and brought him back to the manor house, where Greg and I were by then. They didn't catch Luke Hoyle on the Haseley Hall grounds that night, but they picked him up on the interstate an hour later. He sat tight, but with me as a witness to his killing Uncle Ned, they had more than enough to hold him. They were not, under the circumstances, terribly interested in Uncle Ned's part in the curse on Unicorn Farm, the misuse of muscle relaxant, and the transmission of killer bacteria. But they were like kids in a candy store over the names attached to the IOUs and other documents we'd found in Uncle Ned's bookshelf hiding place. They belonged to racketeers the FBI had been trying to jail for years.

Tim and I had been right in what we'd guessed— the racketeers had wanted to take over Unicorn Farm and its prime assets (the stallions), and had seen in Uncle Ned's weakness for alcohol and gambling a way to do it. It would probably be years before the criminal prosecutions were all completed, but in the meantime Luke Hoyle was behind bars.

Rowena and I never did get to the Lexington Ball that year.

She was in the hospital for two weeks. By the time she came home, bluegrass and flowers were a splendor in the meadow, I was putting the pieces of Unicorn Farm back together with the help of Tom Beech and Greg Stahl, Tapestry was back in training for the Derby, and both Cyrus and Uncle Ned had been buried beneath the willow tree not far from the grave markers of past Unicorn Farm champions. Home burial used to be the custom on old plantations, and Rowena and I agreed the two men would have liked it. They both loved horses; they both, in the last analysis, loved Unicorn Farm.

We had a memorial service for them in the stable yard two days after Rowena came home. She was there in a wheelchair, with Greg beside her, as he'd been almost every minute since the substitute horse attacked. Tim was with me. He was dressed, for the first time since I'd known him, in formal riding clothes, with his grandfather's racing colors in his buttonhole. I was dressed that way, too, and I wore Unicorn Farm's.

The night Rowena had come home from the

hospital, she'd given me the small brass unicorn figure from her desk. "Dad gave this to me as a private family trophy—a reward for valor. I want you to have it for the same reason." It sat on my bureau after that, and it didn't seem sinister anymore.

Rowena and I didn't get to the Lexington Ball, but we did get to the Derby. Rowena was still in a wheelchair, but Greg had us all driven to Louisville in style in a stretch limousine long enough to accommodate her cast. The jouncing ride must have hurt her like the devil, but the devil himself couldn't have kept her home. There was no longer a shadow on Unicorn Farm.

Enough of the truth about the bacteria cultures and their use had leaked out, and traveled the horse breeders' grapevine, for everyone to know the curse was lifted. We were already almost fully booked for Beauvais's stud services during next year's breeding season. Since everyone knew by now about the part Beauvais had played in the capture of Luke Hoyle; it seemed to have proved the continuing value of his bloodline in the eyes of the racing community.

Tapestry was running as Haseley Hall's entry in the Kentucky Derby. Because he'd been "dead" and, during that missing period, had been out of training, Tapestry hadn't run in the earlier spring races as Greg had planned. Ever since I'd found Tapestry, decidedly alive, his training had been resumed under high security and high secrecy. He'd be racing in the Derby as an unknown quantity. According to Tim, rumors had leaked out to make Tapestry a dark-horse favorite. A few days ago, on the Haseley Hall track, he'd matched Beau's Derby record. If Tapestry did well today, Unicorn Farm's future would be assurd.

In her wheelchair, in the Haseley Hall box at Churchill Downs racetrack on Derby day, Rowena held court like a queen.

A rock-sized diamond sparkled on her left hand. She had accepted it from Greg the night before, and there would be a wedding (and probably a European honeymoon) as soon as her leg had healed. While they were traveling the international racing circuit, *I* would be having my heart's desire, a summer of learning to run Unicorn Farm. And Tim would be there with me. Just as he was with me at the Derby, having dreams of his own of a future Derby win for his grandfather's colors.

Unicorn Farm had no entry in the Derby this year, but someday soon . . . someday, perhaps, we'd have Starfire.

The crowd began to settle in its seats as the time for the race approached. There were only Greg and Rowena, Tim and me in the box now. Rowena reached for the program she hadn't yet had time to read, but Greg stopped her.

"Before you read that, you'd better read this first. I'm afraid, otherwise, your cast might become a lethal weapon." He took a legal document from his pocket and held it out. Rowena opened it, puzzled. Then she gasped. "Gregory Stahl! How you dared!"

"You flatly refused to syndicate Tapestry or to allow me to be co-owner of him with you, but there was no law that said once I'd bought him *I* couldn't set up a syndicate and make *you* part owner," Greg said smugly. "You and I—or rather, Haseley Hall and Unicorn Farm—will own the majority of shares between us. After today, we will put the others on the market. They should be worth a great deal. If

Tapestry should win the Derby, he will have done so wearing Haseley Hall colors, but Rowena Drake will be one of the owners of record. Not that the name of Rowena Drake needs any further luster."

He leaned over and kissed her, effectively forestalling anything she could say.

The horses were being led to the starting gate. Somewhere an announcer was broadcasting the names, bloodlines, and owners. *Tapestry, sired by Beauvais. Bred at Unicorn Farm. Raced in Haseley Hall colors by Gregory Stahl and Rowena Drake . . .*

The sun was golden in the sky, touching with magic the familiar turrets of the grandstand, the state and national flags. A hush fell as the band began to play the state's anthem. "My Old Kentucky Home" . . . A lump formed in my throat, and I felt Tim's arm come around me.

All at once that childhood memory of Unicorn Farm came back to me, so clearly. Sunlight, joyfulness, and peace. The peace was back again now, and so was the joy. I put my hand over Tim's, and his fingers tightened on mine. Love was a gamble, and often—how well I knew by now—love could mean loss. But it was worth it. Trust was a gamble, *life* was a gamble, but both were worth it. No matter what the cost.

And that, I thought happily, was what made horseraces.

ABOUT THE AUTHOR

NORMA **J**OHNSTON is the author of over sixty books for adults and young adults, including the highly praised Carlisle Chronicles series. Ms. Johnston has many different interests, from theater, gourmet cooking, and history to psychology, folksongs, and computers. She has traveled extensively around the world, from Europe to the Middle East.

Ms. Johnston's varied career has included being a teacher, actress and play director, boutique owner, and free-lance editor. About her highly successful writing career, she says, "Why do I write? Because I have things that I must say—in person, over a pot of tea before the fire, on stage, in print—and I can no more hold back from saying them than I can cease to breathe."

Her most recent work includes another gothic mystery for Bantam Starfire, *The Watcher in the Mist*.

Readers can write to her at Dryden Harris St. John, Inc., 103 Godwin Avenue, Midland Park, NJ, 07432.

The Carlisle Chronicles

Three tales of the Carlisle Family starring 15-year-old Jess Carlisle

Jess Carlisle's father works for the government and the family has moved around a lot. Maybe that's why roots and "family" are so important to her—she's the only Carlisle who doesn't enjoy being footloose.

☐ **CARLISLE'S HOPE: CARLISLE CHRONICLES #1** (25467 • $2.50)
When she delves into Carlisle family history for a school project, Jess uncovers an old secret that forever changes the way she views her family, and herself.

☐ **TO JESS WITH LOVE AND MEMORIES: CARLISLE CHRONICLES #2** (25882 • $2.50)
When Jess discovers she was adopted, she reacts with bitterness and hurt, until she learns the real truth about her birth.

☐ **CARLISLE'S ALL: CARLISLE CHRONICLES #3** (26139 • $2.50)
Mr. Carlisle is taken hostage in the Middle East and the Carlisles must all pull together to find a way to free him.